CLEAN GETAWAY

CLEAN GETAWAY

NIC STONE

Crown Books for Young Readers

New York

Text copyright © 2020 by Logolepsy Media Inc.
Jacket and interior illustrations copyright © 2020 by Dawud Anyabwile

All rights reserved. Published in the United States by Crown Books for Young Readers, an imprint of Random House Children's Books, a division of Penguin Random House LLC, New York.

Crown and the colophon are registered trademarks of Penguin Random House LLC.

Visit us on the Web! rhcbooks.com

Educators and librarians, for a variety of teaching tools, visit us at RHTeachersLibrarians.com

Library of Congress Control Number: 2019946322
ISBN 978-1-9848-9297-3 (trade) — ISBN 978-1-9848-9298-0 (lib. bdg.) — ISBN 978-1-9848-9299-7 (ebook)

Printed in the United States of America
10 9 8 7 6 5 4 3 2
First Edition

For Jason Reynolds.
Who continues to raise the bar.

Each of us is more than
the worst thing we've ever done.

—Bryan Stevenson

Quite a Ways to Go

It might sound silly, but to William "Scoob" Lamar, the WELCOME TO ALABAMA THE BEAUTIFUL sign looks . . . well, *beautiful*. Not as beautiful as his best friend Shenice Lockwood in her yellow sundress, but beautiful enough to make Scoob tip his head back, close his eyes, and sigh into the breeze blowing through the open passenger-side window of G'ma's Winnebago.

Exhale Dad's lockdown. Inhale the sweet fragrance of freedom. Which smells like pine mixed with a little bit of truck exhaust.

"You all right over there, Scoob-a-doob?" G'ma

says from the driver's seat. She's propped up on the gingham-covered foam wedge she uses to see over the steering wheel, pale, polka-dotted little hands perfectly positioned at ten and two. She's only four feet, eleven inches tall, G'ma is.

Hearing his *full* nickname makes Scoob cringe. G'ma gave it to him when he was five years old and obsessed with an old cartoon he used to watch at her house about a dog who liked to solve mysteries. G'ma thought it was *just too adorable!* that he couldn't pronounce *Scooby-Doo*. And because

Shenice was G'ma's neighbor, she picked up on the nickname and started using it at school. So it stuck.

Well, the *Scoob* part did. Which is fine. Kinda *cool*, even.

Scoob-a-doob, though?

"G'ma," he says, "you mind if we stick to *Scoob*? The rest is a little . . . babyish. No offense," he adds.

"Oh, none taken!" G'ma says. "My apologies, Mr. Scoob."

"I mean . . . you can drop the *mister*, too," Scoob goes on.

This makes G'ma laugh.

Which makes Scoob smile. He'd never tell anybody, but there's really no sound in the world he loves more than his grandmother's barking laughter. Dad's not a fan; says it "grates" on him because it's the one reminder of G'ma's past smoking days "and potential future lung cancer," but it reminds Scoob of elementary school days playing card games she taught him that he wasn't supposed to know the rules for—like Texas Hold'em and blackjack. Even now, it blows Scoob's mind that a harsh, booming sound like that could come out of a person as little as G'ma.

"I mean it, though," she says. "You feeling all right? I'm not driving too fast, am I?" She kicks him a wrinkly wink.

Now Scoob's the one laughing. He looks up from the brand-new road map she handed him once they were both settled and seat-belted: according to the speedometer, the brand-new Winnebago he and G'ma are in has a max speed of 120 miles per hour, but G'ma has yet to push the needle to 60. "Definitely not too fast, G'ma. Though I do wonder if there's a *minimum*-speed-limit law you're breaking."

"Oh you hush," she says. "Speaking of which, you never said if you liked my new sweet ride or not. That's what you kids call it these days, right? A sweet ride?" She says it in a way that makes her sound like a smarmy used-car salesman with oil-slicked hair.

Scoob chuckles and shakes his head. Then he peeks over his shoulder into the back.

Truthfully, when G'ma popped up out of the blue and asked if Scoob wanted to "go on a little adventure," he was too geeked at the thought of a loophole in his punishment to give much thought to anything else, their destination included. Especially when she said he'd "probably miss a couple days of school." (Bonus!) He finished item three—*empty the dishwasher*—on the to-do list Dad left for him on the kitchen whiteboard every day, and grabbed his suitcase. Then, after scribbling Dad a quick note about being with G'ma "for the night," Scoob hightailed it out of the house as fast as his off-brand-sneaker-clad feet would carry him. Even left his phone at home.

Largely so Dad can't call him, but he won't tell G'ma that.

The suitcase had been sitting in Scoob's closet for a month. Dad promised Scoob a trip to St. Simons Island this year—Scoob's *first* choice was Universal Studios, but Dad said Scoob was "too old for all that." (He'd been "too young" the previous year, but whatever.) So Scoob packed up according to Dad's specifications three days before they were supposed to depart.

Except they didn't go. Scoob got in trouble at school, and voilà: trip canceled. Lockdown commenced. Spring break ruined before it could begin.

Scoob hadn't been able to bring himself to unpack the bag, so he hid it. Now he can see it sitting on the seat of the dining booth in G'ma's *new sweet ride*.

Scoob was in such a rush to get out, it didn't *fully* *click* that he and G'ma weren't in the MINI Cooper until she asked him to get out of his seat—while the vehicle was in motion—and "grab a GPS from the fridge" (that's *Grandma Protein Shake,* otherwise known as *Ensure*) for her.

Fridge? Scoob thought, lightbulb slowly illuminating.

That's when he looked behind him for the first time. And almost choked on the gum that shot down his throat when he gasped.

"Ain't he handsome?" G'ma said, smacking the dashboard twice. "Brand spankin' new, this fella. I've decided to call him Senior after your late grandfather. He and I had a Winnebago back in the day before your dad was born and your G'pop—" She paused. Then: "Anyway, I ain't gettin' any younger. Sold my house and bought this baby—"

"You *sold your house?*" Scoob said, stunned.

"Sure did. Fetched a pretty penny for it, too. God

6

bless home equity and hipsters lookin' to 'revitalize' or whatever the heck they're calling it."

"Wow." (Was there anything else he could've said? She sold her *house!*)

"Well, ya gonna get me a GPS or not?"

Scoob gulped, removed his seat belt, and made his way to the back. Dad would've breathed fire and shot smoke out of his ears if he'd been around to see.

As he opened the for-*real,* for-real fridge—with separate freezer!—G'ma gave him a rundown of "Senior's" features. "You see those lights above your head?"

Scoob looked up. "Yeah . . ."

"Those are *LEDs,*" she said. "Real state-of-the art! There's also a microwave, a *two*-burner cook-top, and *two* ultra-HD TVs where you can watch anything! Rated PG-13 or lower, that is."

Scoob rolled his eyes.

G'ma pushed on. "Bathroom's there to the left of the mini-pantry—got a flushing toilet and a shower! And that dining booth you see there? Doubles as a bed. And speaking of beds, there's one in the rear for me, and one for you right above the cab here.

There's a window up there and everything, kiddo!"

Scoob could hear the proud smile in her voice.

Which made him smile too. Despite the fact that she'd called him kiddo.

As he grabbed the drink for G'ma and saw that the fridge was fully stocked, Scoob realized he'd never again play on the old tire swing in G'ma's backyard or kick back on the old window seat in the attic with his favorite book. When it hit him that *this,* this bizarre truck that contained everything a person needs to live, this *thing* was now G'ma's house?

Creepy.

G'ma's fingers do a tap dance on the steering wheel, pulling him back into the present, and he takes a deep breath and lets his eyes continue to roam around the open space behind him. It's so weird to him that if he has to pee, all he's gotta do is walk like fifteen feet to the little bathroom. And it *flushes*? Where does the stuff even go? It's not like they're connected to a sewer. And what about the dirty dish and shower water?

G'ma's house had one of those old-school bathtubs with the fancy metal feet, and Scoob secretly loved to get in with one or two of the lemon-sized balls G'ma would buy that would fizz up like Alka-Seltzer and turn the bath all kinds of wild colors. *Plop! Fizzzzzzz* . . . and the water would be blue and kind of shimmery. Like taking a soak in the galaxy.

This RV doesn't have a tub. So no more galaxy baths.

His gaze catches on the kitchenette thingy as he faces forward. Which just adds to his sudden sadness. He can't imagine G'ma making her blue-ribbon-winning cast-iron French toast—first pan-toasted, then baked in the pan for a few minutes for extra crispiness on the outside—on that rinky-dink cooktop thingy. No more extra-sweet Arnold Palmers on the porch swing. No more reading in front of the fire.

In all honesty, the RV gives Scoob the willies. But of course he can't tell G'ma that. Not when she's so excited about it.

"Well?" she says, taking her baby-blue eyes off the road to look at him. Second only to Shenice's honey-brown ones, G'ma's got the prettiest eyes Scoob's ever seen. "What do you think, kiddo?"

Scoob traces the handle of his door and gulps

down his true feelings. "I think it's great, G'ma!" he says with forced enthusiasm.

Whether or not she can tell he's lying, Scoob doesn't know.

"Good," she says. "Settle on in. We've got quite a ways to go."

ROUTE 2

Pay the Bill

The trouble really started six months back during those weird three weeks of school between Thanksgiving and winter break. Scoob's got no idea why, but over the course of that stretch, Bryce Benedict— a kid Scoob *used* to be friends with ("until he started playing 'footyball' and got too big for his britches," G'ma likes to say)—started picking on Shenice's little brother, Drake.

Drake has epilepsy—which was never a big deal until Bryce's antics began.

Things started pretty light: Bryce would make unnecessary detours past Scoob, Shenice, and Drake's table in the cafeteria to tap Drake on the back of the head as he'd shout " 'Sup, Drakey-Drake?" loud enough for the whole room to hear.

After a few days of this, the tapping turned to shoving, turned to smacking. There was one morning Bryce hit so hard, Drake cried out in pain. The nearest teacher hadn't been paying attention—if she had been, Bryce probably wouldn't have done it. But when she turned to see what'd happened, Bryce was gone and Drake said nothing.

So no one else said anything either.

The following day, Bryce cornered Drake in the hallway to taunt him. Scoob arrived just as Drake's arms jerked of their own accord and he dropped all the books he was holding.

Of course old Bryce found this—and Shenice's protective punch in the chest—hilarious.

He shoved Drake's shoulder—hard—and walked off just as Scoob rushed over to help Shenice and Drake with the books. As they gathered everything, Scoob could tell Drake was fighting with everything he had to keep from crying.

Shenice *was* crying.

For the first time in his life, Scoob experienced a

violent urge: he wanted to smack Bryce upside his fat head.

"Whew," G'ma says as Scoob relays the story to her over an early dinner. They're at a place called DamnYankees, and the lemon pepper wings truly are *smokin'*, just like the menu says. Decor's a bit . . . country: rodeo posters and horseshoes and cowboy hats all over the walls, lassos and saddles hanging from the ceiling. There's even a mounted bull's head, massive horns menacingly outstretched. "Can't blame ya, Scoob-a-doob," G'ma continues.

Scoob sighs, grateful *some* grown-up in his life seems to understand. "I knew you'd get it, G'ma." Because she always does.

"What'd Drake have to say?" G'ma asks.

"He shrugged it off. Said 'He's just being a bully.' Which made me even madder."

"I bet. Hard seeing someone you care about brush that kinda thing off, ain't it?"

Scoob nods. "It really is."

As the days wore on, Bryce's taunting got more intense. One day after school, Shenice confided in

Scoob that Drake hadn't been sleeping real well. That he'd been having bad dreams, and she was pretty sure they had to do with Bryce picking on him. That he'd been having more seizures despite taking his medicine like he was supposed to.

"That's when I started noticing that Drake would, like . . . blank out at random times," Scoob says to G'ma. "There was even a day someone was talking to him at the lunch table and he didn't respond. Just sat staring straight ahead."

People had looked around at each other and started whispering.

And on Drake sat, perfectly still. Blinking. Blinking. Blinking.

"Bryce passed by and hit him, and Drake's whole body lurched forward like a board. Which Bryce thought was *hilarious*." Scoob's eyes narrow as the anger begins to simmer again. "He pointed one of his fat, pink fingers at Drake and laughed. Imitated Drake's blinks. 'Looks like he's having one of his "seizures,"' he said. Did air quotes and everything." Scoob shakes his head.

G'ma shakes hers, too.

"*Then* he said, 'Too bad it's not the type where

14

he shakes and his tongue falls out . . .' And he stuck his big, ugly tongue out and pretended to convulse. Shenice jumped up and said something I won't repeat, and then Bryce looked at *her* like the evil villains do in the cartoons just before they hurt people. When he took a step toward her, I—" Scoob sighs. "I lost it, G'ma. Just kinda . . . snapped."

Scoob will never forget hearing Ms. Manasmith gasp as he leapt from his seat, hopped the table, and tackled Bryce.

Then they were on the floor. Bryce on his back. Scoob on top of him.

Punching.

Punching.

Punching.

Scoob's got no idea how long he punched. He just knows that at some point, one of the punches failed to connect because he was flying up, up, up. And by the time his surroundings came into focus, there was no longer a youngish white lady staring at him, but a little old brown-skinned dude.

Mr. Armand. The principal of Casey M. Weeks Magnet Middle School.

Soon, *that* dude was joined by a BIG, slightly

lighter-brown-skinned dude: Dr. James Robert Lamar Jr.

Scoob's father.

"And that was the beginning of the end," Scoob says to G'ma as he rips another hunk of lemony-peppery meat from a chicken leg.

"The end of what exactly?" G'ma's eating raw oysters. Scoob shuts his eyes as she picks up a shell and tips the glob-of-gross into her now-snaggletooth mouth. She removed her "partial." The thought of the false teeth currently chillin' in their purple glitter container inside G'ma's purse almost grosses Scoob out as much as the oysters.

Scoob shudders and takes a sip of sweet tea to clear his head. "Sorry, what was the question?"

G'ma smiles. "You said the fight with Bryce the bonehead was 'the beginning of the end.' The end of *what*?"

"Oh," Scoob says, lowering his eyes to his near-empty plate. "The end of . . . well, Dad's faith in me, I guess."

Not that Dad would *listen* to Scoob when Scoob tried to explain why he did it. "You think a police officer will care about you 'defending a friend'

when they toss you in jail for aggravated assault?"
Dad said on the way home from school to begin
Scoob's three-day suspension. "You can't react vi-
olently to someone else's words. Especially someone like Bryce. When boys like *you*"—he pointed
to the brown back of Scoob's hand—"hit boys like
him"—he opened his own hand and pointed to his
pale palm—"the punishment is harsher and the fall-
out infinitely worse, William."

Scoob will never forget Dad's look of disappointment.

"Seems a tad extreme, don't you think?" G'ma
says, plucking Scoob back to the present.

He shakes his head. "Not really. He used to tell
me he had faith in me all the time, but now he acts
like I'm some hardened delinquent. It's like he
thinks there's no hope for me or something. Won't
even look me in the eye anymore. Especially since
that *other* incident."

"The one with the computers."

"Yep."

G'ma doesn't press further. Which Scoob is
thankful for. He really doesn't want to get into that
right now.

He takes another swig of sweet tea to swallow the little ball that's risen in his throat. This is the first time he's spoken aloud about the way Dad's been to him lately.

Kinda makes him want to cry.

But he won't.

Though he can totally feel G'ma looking at him, and he knows from the way the hairs on the back of his neck are rising, she's doing that thing where she tries to see inside his head. If he looks at her now, she'll see all the other mess—Scoob's frustration over the fact that Bryce wasn't punished, his annoyance that all the teachers look at him like he's a lit stick of dynamite now *despite* the fact that Bryce is still terrorizing people (though not Drake anymore), his anger over the unfairness of the whole situation—swirling around behind Scoob's eyes, and she'll drag it all out of him.

But he doesn't want to tell her any of that.

Right now Scoob just wants to get back in G'ma's fancy new drivable home and GO.

Go, and never ever look back.

He pulls himself up straight and lifts his chin.

That's when he notices an older white man in a baseball cap a few tables over looking between him and G'ma like they're some alien beings. Yeah, kids at school used to ask questions when they'd see Scoob and G'ma together—he's black and she's white—but this feels different. Less about curiosity and more . . . disdainful.

And that guy's not the only one: bouncing his eyes around the room, Scoob realizes a *bunch* of people are looking at him and G'ma funny. One lady he makes eye contact with openly sneers at him like he's done something wrong.

Like he *is* something wrong, even.

It's the same way Dad looked at him when he stepped into Mr. Armand's office that first time after the fight.

His hand tightens around his damp glass of tea. Which he'd really like to pick up and lob at the woman. Give her a *reason* to look at him the way she is.

G'ma's warm hand squeezes Scoob's other one, which is resting on the table in a fist. He locks eyes with her and she smiles. His chest unclenches a little.

"Whattya say we blow this popsicle stand, huh?" she asks him. "We've eaten our fill. Now time to eat some road."

Scoob nods and grins. "Sounds disgusting, G'ma. But okay."

As they make their way outside, G'ma turns to him and says, "These small towns are really something, aren't they? *Bass ackwards,* as your G'pop used to say. But that's all right . . ."

She doesn't say anything else, and Scoob doesn't respond. But as they pull away from Damn Yankees it hits him: he's pretty sure G'ma didn't pay the bill.

Never Seen Before

By the time Scoob and G'ma have "set up camp"—aka parked the RV at their "campsite" in the hills of Alabama's Cheaha State Park and connected G'ma's fancy water filter and hose to the spigot at their campsite so they won't run through what's in the RV's fresh water tank—the drooping sun has turned the sky the colors of Scoob's favorite fruit: a sweet Georgia peach.

In fact, Scoob snagged a few from the bowl on his kitchen table and stuffed them in his backpack while on the way out the door with G'ma this afternoon.

Come to think of it, that bowl was empty when Scoob left for school this morning. He'd eaten the last two the night before as he sat through a show Dad was making him watch on National Geographic about the fiercely territorial nature of hippos.

Which means Dad refilled it at some point. For Scoob. Because Dad doesn't like peaches. Always says they're "the pits," and then he laughs at his corny dad-joke.

When had Dad done that?

"Ready for a little adventurin', Scoob-a-doob—whoops!" G'ma giggles as she approaches the picnic table where Scoob's sitting, drawing pine trees all around the spot where he circled the park they're at on the map G'ma gave him.

Well, at least that's what he *was* doing before he got all googly-eyed over the peachy sunset.

"Sorry," G'ma goes on. "Forgot I'm supposed to drop the *a-doob* now that you're practically a grown man." She winks at him and pats the top of his head.

"Aww, come on, G'ma."

"How about *you* come on," she says. "We've got a short hike, and I wanna get to the peak of this mountain before the sun disappears. You carry this." She sets a wooden box on the picnic table in front of Scoob. The hinged lid is ornately carved, and it's about the size of his school math book.

He freezes.

G'ma's treasure box.

He looks over the loops and swirls and leaves etched into the top. The box is a reddish brown, and he knows it's made of rosewood because G'ma told

him years ago when he first noticed it sitting up on her mantel.

It's the one thing that was always off-limits in G'ma's house. Scoob's never even touched it before.

Okay, that's a lie. As soon as he was tall enough— age seven-ish?—he reached up and touched the lacquered side just because . . . well, because he wasn't supposed to touch it.

Looking at it now, though, Scoob gets smacked again by the fact that he'll never see it on the mantel again. Never see the inside of G'ma's *house* again.

"Stick it down in your knapsack," she says.

Which . . . she wants him to carry her treasure box in his backpack? Up a mountain? What if she's only taking it up there to toss it over the edge or something? Rid herself of it like she did her *home*. Scoob doesn't know if he could handle that.

He gulps. "We're . . . uhh . . . taking it on a hike?"

"That we are," she says. "Now scoot your boot." And she walks off without another word.

So okay. Watching the sun go down all the way from the highest point in Alabama is kinda neat. In fact,

Scoob's looking forward to getting back down to the campsite so he can add a sunset in the margin of his road map. "Well, ain't that something?" G'ma says from beside Scoob. They're in the observation room at the top of an old tower, which the pamphlet says was built in 1934.

"Can you believe Bunker Tower had been standing for nine years by the time I was born?" G'ma says. "It's magnificent!"

"It's something, all right." Scoob gives a wary glance around the interior. He sure hopes it doesn't suddenly decide to crumble.

"I've been waiting fifty-one years to see this view, Scoob-a-doob," G'ma says.

That gets Scoob's attention. "Fifty-one *years*?"

"Yep."

Scoob shifts his gaze back out across the landscape. "Why didn't you come before now?"

"Wasn't ready."

No idea what that means . . .

"Really not ready now, but the world ain't slowing its spin."

"Okay," Scoob says.

"Go ahead and open the box."

The box. Scoob forgot he was even carrying it, though, come to think of it, his shoulders are hurting from the extra weight. He takes a deep breath, shrugs the bag down, and drops to a knee. Unzips and pulls out the box.

Stares at it.

"It won't bite ya," G'ma says. "Well . . . at least I don't think it will." She smiles and pats the top of his head.

Scoob runs a thumb over the brassy latch. What if what's inside isn't all that exciting? It'll ruin the whole thing. Scoob would never admit it to anyone, but there are books he's never finished because he liked imagining all the things that *could* happen. Knowing what *does* happen would take the fun out of it.

Scoob's mom pops into his mind unbidden. Her name is Destiny, but . . . well, he's never met her. He knows she left when he was a baby because she wasn't ready to be a mom—Dad told him that part—but he doesn't know much else because the one time he asked about her, Dad made it clear he didn't want to talk about it.

So he just makes things up. Though he'd never

tell anyone. In his mind she's been everything from an astronaut like Mae Jemison—Dad's an aeronautical engineer and has a picture of Mae in her space suit on the wall in his office—to a brown lady Indiana Jones going on treasure-hunting adventures.

She's an unsolved mystery. His personal treasure box.

And now he's holding *G'ma's* treasure box. He's imagined it containing everything from his granddad's ashes to the bones of some beloved pet to heaps of glittering jewels. He imagines the vines carved into the lid coming to life like wooden snakes, lashing at him the moment he tries to lift it.

"Well?" G'ma says.

Scoob closes his eyes, flicks the latch, and shoves the lid up. Peeks inside through one barely cracked eye.

The contents are . . . unexpected.

"Voilà. My greatest treasure."

There's an old radio tucked up against the left side, plus some matchbooks and a few postcards. There are guidebooks to places Scoob's never heard of before, and some newspaper clippings; a series of weathered road maps not unlike the one G'ma gave him, a small photo album, and a little green book called . . . *Travelers' Green Book*. "For Vacation Without Aggravation," the cover says in bold white letters.

The Green Book is from 1963. As in not even this century.

"Wow, *this* thing sure stirs up some memories," G'ma says, grunting as she bends at the waist to remove the Green Book. It's about the same size as the postcards.

Scoob watches her flip through it like she does a deck of cards before dealing Texas Hold'em. "What is it?" he asks.

"Somethin' that helped keep a lotta folks like your G'pop—and *me,* for that matter—alive back in the day."

Scoob zeroes in on the cover. It features an image of two women—he can't tell what race they are; everything is tinted green (surprise, surprise)—

leaning over a small boat beneath a sky full of fluffy clouds. "Really?"

"Mmhmm." She sighs and taps the book against her palm. "Hate to tell you this, Scoob-a-doob, but travel around this grand ol' USA wasn't always a safe thing for people who look like you. This was a meeeeeean place back when your G'pop and I were young, and that book existed to let Negro travelers know which hotels and such would accept them as customers. There are even some *other* countries in there. Here." She hands Scoob the book. "You hold on to it. Might learn ya somethin'."

Scoob flips the book to check out the back, then shoves it into his pocket without a word.

"Now grab the Alabama map, if you will, please."

He riffles through the rest of the stuff, looking for what she requested, and finds it beneath a napkin with a circular stain on it. Probably from a cup of coffee. It's weathered and pamphlet-style, ALABAMA printed vertically in bold letters on the front.

"Open it up."

There's a route highlighted—broken up by circled

spots with handwritten notes scribbled over them—that cuts straight across from the Georgia/Alabama line to Alabama's midpoint in Birmingham, and then veers southwest to the state's opposite border.

"Can you see what's circled just below and to the right of Anniston?"

Scoob holds the map a little closer. "Cheaha State Park." *The highest point in Alabama* is scrawled above the spot of green.

In awe, Scoob looks all around him. Then at G'ma. Who nods. Just once. "Fifty-one years," she says.

Then she begins to sob like Scoob's never seen before.

Life Pollution

On the way back down the mountain, Scoob's so focused on G'ma—that was his first time ever seeing her cry, and she told him a *lot* about his grandfather—he trips on a tree root and comes down hard on a small rock partially buried in the dirt of the walking trail.

"My word, are you all right, Scoob-a-doob?" G'ma says, reaching to help him up.

"I'm fine, G'ma." Scoob dusts the woodland debris from his clothes and tries to play it off.

They continue walking, Scoob's mind swirling. While G'ma sobbed over the sunset, it hit Scoob:

his grandfather had needed a *book* that listed "safe" places to do something as simple as get gas back in the day.

Because he was black.

By the time they get back to G'ma's new sweet ride, there's a dull ache in his right arm, but all he can think about is the phrase *For Vacation Without Aggravation* and that boat on calm water beneath those fluffy clouds.

That is, until they're inside the RV where the light is brighter.

"Oh!" G'ma shouts, startling Scoob. "Oh, oh, OH! That needs to be cleaned immediately! Come, come!"

When Scoob looks at his arm and sees the lines of drying blood that have run down over his hand from a nasty-looking cut near his elbow, the dull ache explodes into a burning throb. "Oh."

"Put that bag down," G'ma orders, and as soon as he does, she's dragging him over to the kitchenette sink by his good arm and washing her hands. Then she shoves his arm underneath the warm water.

It takes the force of Thor to keep his jaw clenched so he doesn't scream like a giant baby.

In fact, said *jaw* is aching by the time G'ma fin-ishes with the rubbing alcohol and weird-colored Betadine and bag balm (for chapped cow udders?). By the time the nickel-sized cut is bandaged, Scoob's exhausted.

He collapses into the dining booth and looks up at the over-cab bunk where he's supposed to sleep.

What if he rolls off?

"Hot cocoa?" G'ma says.

Scoob shakes his head. "No thanks, G'ma. Think I'm gonna call it a night."

"All right, well, before ya go . . ." She unzips Scoob's backpack and pulls the treasure box out. Digs around and stretches a photo out to him.

"That's your G'pop," she says. "Keep that with your Green Book."

Of course now he can't sleep.

Between the photo and the book, Scoob's thoughts are whipping around faster than a load of clothes in their front-loading washer during the spin cycle, something he typically loves watching but is queasy about now.

In the photo, "G'pop" is leaned up against what looks like a white box on wheels with a big green W up under the driver window. Scoob is guessing this is the Winnebago G'ma mentioned earlier, though it's clearly the great-great-grandparent model of the motor home where Scoob is currently stretched out in his bed, staring at this picture.

Scoob brings the photo closer to his face. G'pop was tall and string-beany, a shade darker than Scoob, so two shades darker than Dad. Scoob can *see* his dear old dad all up in G'pop's face—though Dad is currently older than G'pop was in this picture, so it's almost like looking at a *younger* Dad—

and it makes Scoob wonder if this is what *he'll* look like in a decade and a half or so. People are always telling him he's the "spitting image" of Dad, which is kinda nasty, but whatever.

It's weird, looking at his grandfather. In almost twelve years, this is the first photo Scoob's ever seen of the guy. He'd never really even heard G'ma talk about the dude before tonight. Which, now that he thinks about it, probably isn't normal? He never questioned it before because Dad always said the old man had been a "nonentity" since before Dad was actually born.

But from the beans G'ma spilled all over the top

of Alabama, Scoob now knows that James Lamar Sr. was quite the *entity*. Especially to her, his darling wife, Ruby Jean.

What G'ma told him through her tears (and a little snot and drool, too): in 1968 she and G'pop bought an RV. They planned to drive from their home in Georgia across five southern states and straight into Mexico. On her maps—which are *all* in the treasure chest—G'ma marked the stuff she wanted to see along the way. But they'd had to skip most of her chosen sites because G'ma is a white lady but "your G'pop was a *Negro,* as we used to say back then."

Cheaha Mountain had been the first stop she wanted to make, but when they got to the turnoff for the drive to the top, G'pop told her there was no way they'd be able to park up there without people messing with them.

Scoob puts the picture aside and picks up the green booklet. Reads the words just inside the front cover—*Assured Protection for the Negro Traveler*—skims the intro page, which outlines state-by-state "statutes on discrimination as they apply to public accommodations or recreation," then flips to the *Alabama* section. Scoob knows Anniston is the closest city to where they are now, and it's not in the book at all.

Which means there was *nowhere* safe for black people to stay around here back when G'ma and G'pop took their trip.

So they drove past.

This journey Scoob and G'ma are on now? According to her, "It's my chance at redemption. To finish what your G'pop and I started fifty-one years ago." And while she doesn't go into detail, she does tell Scoob they never made it to Mexico.

G'ma lets out a gigantic *snort* from her curtained-off "bedroom" at the opposite end of the RV, and Scoob switches back to the picture and holds it in the light coming through the small window. G'pop just looks so . . . *chill*. Real happy, smiley type of guy, despite having on plaid booty-shorts hiked up to his belly button that *cannot* be comfortable.

Dad told Scoob G'pop was a jewel thief who went to prison shortly before Dad's birth. And G'pop died there.

In prison.

Really, the only time Dad ever brings G'pop up is

to say, "No son of mine will become a low-life criminal like my father!" when he's going off on Scoob about some "infraction" or another.

But G'pop doesn't *look* like a terrible guy. And after hearing G'ma talk about her "beloved *Jimmy Senior*," Scoob wonders if Dad got it all wrong. Dad himself even said he'd never *met* G'pop.

What if G'pop really wasn't all that bad? G'ma obviously loved him enough to marry him, and Dad's always saying, "William, your grandmother is a queen. Never forget it." That has to mean something, doesn't it?

Thoughts of Scoob's mom slip back into his head like those long stringy clouds, see-through and not fully formed but visible. Dad doesn't know it, but Scoob's aware she's tried to contact Scoob before. Just before he turned ten, she left a voice mail that Scoob accidentally heard while trying to call Drake on Dad's phone.

He still remembers every word:

> James, it's Destiny. A friend of mine helped me find your phone number . . . hope that's okay. I know

it's been a long time, but . . . well, I'm better now and . . . I need to see my baby boy, James. Please.

And she left a number.

By the time Dad woke up from the nap he was taking, Scoob had listened to the message sixteen times. And he *knows* Dad knows he heard it because there's no way to make a listened-to voice mail "new" again.

And try as he might, after hearing her voice, he'd been unable to slip back into his imaginings of her that time. He watched Dad for *days*, just waiting for him to say, "Son, I think it's time you met your mother," but it never happened. Days became weeks, and Dad didn't say a word.

By the time Scoob worked up the courage to just call the number she left—twenty-seven days later, on the day *after* his double-digit birthday—*ten* meant he had to be braver, right?—he got a *the number you have dialed has been disconnected or is no longer in service* message.

He said something to Dad then: "Hey, Dad, I know my mom called—"

And that's all he got out. Cuz Dad cut him off. "She left, William. She's gone. Absent. Same way my father was. End of story."

But what if it's not? What if there's *more* to the story like there clearly is to G'pop?

Scoob fills his cheeks with air and blows out. Rolls back to his stomach and tucks the picture of G'pop into the Green Book, then shoves both under his pillow. He peeks through the window by his head. The sky looks like somebody took an oceanful of the silvery glitter stuff G'ma sometimes wears on her eyelids when she's "feelin' fancy" and threw it into the air. He had no idea so many stars even existed.

G'ma said they can't see them from Atlanta because there's too much *light pollution*. Tonight, he learned more than he realized there was to know about a guy he'd always been told didn't matter. What else could Scoob not know about in the sky of his existence?

Is there such a thing as *life* pollution?

Run for It

When Scoob wakes up the next morning and climbs down from his bunk, G'ma is gone. He doesn't think much of it: there's coffee in the pot by the sink, a half-done crossword puzzle beside an empty mug, and a plate of green grapes on the dining booth table.

But when he goes to pee and hears rustling and scraping sounds behind the RV—like someone's messing with it—the Green Book and everything G'ma told him about why she and G'pop hadn't stopped here leaps into Scoob's head at the same time his heart leaps up between his ears.

So does that restaurant. DamnYankees. It only took Scoob and G'ma twenty minutes to get to where they are now from there. In addition to eating together despite their different skin tones—which, if you let G'ma tell it, was the cause of the dirty looks they were getting—Scoob is ninety-seven-point-two percent sure he and G'ma dined-and-ditched.

What if someone tailed them up the mountain and decided to wait until morning to strike? Or what if they went to round up some of their buddies before making an approach? Scoob read *To Kill a Mockingbird* in language arts last quarter. He knows how stuff used to go down.

There's a creaking sound and then a thump.

What if they already *have* G'ma?

Scraaaaaape.

He takes a deep breath. Not the time for peeing: who/whatever's back there might hear it. He slips out of the bathroom and over to the window beside G'ma's bed. Pulls the shade back just enough to peek out.

The window is a little bit open, and there's a faint *clang* and then a whispered cussword—in a voice Scoob knows (though he's not sure he's ever heard it use *that* word before).

He pulls the curtain back a little more.

G'ma appears from behind the RV, clad in camo—the kind that looks like a forest floor—from the cap on her head to the top of her orthopedic Velcro sneakers. She's got a rectangular piece of metal tucked under her arm and what looks like a screwdriver in her hand.

Weird.

Scoob watches her scan the surroundings before scurrying along the edge of the woods they're parked against. She disappears behind the trailer parked at the next campsite over.

What the heck?

He lets the curtain drop, too confused to do anything but sit on the bed with his eyebrows furrowed.

At the sound of what has to be a snapping twig or something, Scoob looks out again and sees G'ma tiptoeing back across the clearing. This time he can see what she's carrying: a license plate.

Except it's green. And though Scoob knows he hasn't seen *all* the plates in Georgia, he's pretty sure most of them are white. Dad's sure is. So was the one on G'ma's MINI Cooper. *KAL0627*. He remembers from the time he came down the hill too fast on his Rollerblades, lost control, and smacked his forehead right on the *L0*.

He slumps back on the bed. More noise from behind the RV as (Scoob assumes) G'ma attaches the green plate to the bumper.

He's obviously missing something, right? G'ma wouldn't steal someone else's license plate . . .

The knob on the RV door turns, and Scoob scurries into the bathroom and pulls the door shut. Turns on the shower and sits on the lowered lid of the toilet.

Definitely doesn't have to pee anymore.

There's a knock. "Scoob-a-doob? You all right in there?"

Nope. "I'm good, G'ma."

"Didn't you shower last night, sweetpea?"

Oh right. He's supposed to "be mindful" of his "water use." G'ma told him all about the collection tanks for the (dirty) water they use—including the fact that they have to be emptied by hand.

Gross.

"I'm just about done," he says, whipping his clothes off. Can't come out dry now, can he? "I . . . uhhhh . . . had a sweaty night."

"I see," G'ma says. "Well, I'll get started on our breakfast. Bacon and eggs okay with you?"

"Yep!" What even kind of question is that?

Scoob hops in, does a three-sixty so all of him gets wet, then shuts the water off. He slides open the shower door. Looks around.

Curses under his breath.

"Hey, G'ma?" he shouts, shivering.

"Hmm?" comes the reply.

"Can you pass me my towel?"

G'ma must've changed out of her license-plate-swapping gear (*Did she really swap a license plate?*) while Scoob is "in the shower" because by the time he comes out, she's standing over the cooktop in a neon-orange *jogging suit,* as she calls it. All Scoob knows is every time she moves, it sounds like somebody's ripping a sheet of paper. Well . . . that, and instead of a pile of dead leaves, she now looks like a cotton-ball-topped traffic cone.

It makes him smile. And relax a little. "Nice out-fit, G'ma."

She puts a hand on her hip and gives a little shake. "You know I like to keep it snazzy."

Scoob laughs aloud.

"You go on and have a seat," she says. "I'm just about done with the vittles."

"Vittles?"

"Look it up on that mobile device of yours."

Oh.

"Where is it, by the way? I turned mine on for a spell this morning, and there was a voice message from your dad saying he's been trying to reach us but both of our phones are 'going straight to voice mail,' whatever that means." She waves her hand like the very notion is a nuisance. "Anyhow, it made me real-ize I haven't seen you with your phone in your hand since we left. Which is"—she looks over her shoulder at him, white eyebrows raised—"*odd*, I daresay?"

"Oh. Uh." Scoob gulps. "I left it at home." He scratches the back of his head. *You need a haircut, William,* he imagines Dad saying. "Turned off."

G'ma spins all the way around, mock-gasps, and puts the spatula over her heart.

"Come on, G'ma." Scoob drops his chin as his face gets all warm.

She rotates back to plate the food, then brings it to the table. Scoob closes his eyes and inhales. Smells so good, everything else vanishes from his mind. *Poof.*

"Don't you feel . . ." G'ma's voice shoves everything he doesn't want to think about back into his head. "What's that expression you kids use? *Bucky-naked* without it?"

"Nobody says that, G'ma."

"Well. You know what I mean." She eats a forkful of scrambled cheese eggs. "How will you chat with friends? Play your games? Watch the TubeYou—"

"YouTube."

"Mmhmm." She sips from a fresh cup of coffee. "Exactly."

Did he think about all that before powering the thing down and shoving it beneath his mattress?

Of course.

But Scoob's awareness of the angry call he knew he'd get the moment Dad read his note and realized he'd jetted while grounded made all the stuff he'd be "missing" feel pretty minor.

Though hearing about this voice mail does make him a nervous. Maybe he made the wrong decision leaving the phone at home. "Did you . . . call him back?"

"What's that?" G'ma says.

"Dad. Did you call him back and let him know we're okay?" Why Scoob cares, he can't say. But he does.

"Ah, I'll send him a text," she says. "Though I'm surprised to hear you want me to."

"You are?"

"Yep. You leaving your phone at home makes me think you and I have something in common."

"Oh yeah? What's that?"

She grins and takes her final bite of egg. Leans toward Scoob with a twinkle in her eye. "Looks like we're both trying to make a run for it."

A Good Thing

Scoob doesn't say a whole lot as they hit the road—the green license plate and the words *make a run for it* are too busy playing Ultimate Frisbee with his thoughts for him to speak. But pretty soon, he and G'ma are stopping to refuel the RV and to go number two—nobody wants to empty *that* from the tank—in Birmingham, Alabama.

Once the gas is pumped, the poop is dumped, and they're back strapped in and ready to roll, G'ma suddenly looks . . . troubled.

Like, maybe-about-to-cry kind of troubled.

Which he *really* doesn't want to happen again.

For one, he's already got too much on his head. And for two: it makes him super uncomfortable when G'ma cries because he doesn't know what to *do*. "G'ma? You okay?"

She takes a very deep breath and cranks the engine. "I didn't want to make any real Birmingham stops, but . . . well, we gotta," she says. "There's something you need to see, Scoob-a-doob."

"Uhh . . ." (Not scary at all, right?) "Okay . . ."

As they drive, Scoob can feel the Green Book in his pocket against his right booty cheek. He doesn't remember exactly how many *safe* lodging places were listed in Birmingham, but he's sure he wouldn't need more than one hand to count them. Now he's wishing he'd paid more attention to G'ma's Alabama map. Was something circled there?

Much sooner than Scoob expects, they're pulling into a parking lot between two big brick buildings. G'ma shuts the RV off and moves to get out.

"G'ma, you sure we're allowed to park here?"

"Oh, we won't be long," she replies. "Hop on down."

Scoob does as he's told, and they head toward the building on the left.

"So that"—she points to a building across the street—"I believe is the Birmingham Civil Rights Institute."

"Whoa," Scoob says. The place almost takes up the whole block.

"And this"—they reach the intersection of Sixteenth Street and Sixth Avenue according to the signs on the traffic light posts; and speaking of signs, there's a really old-looking one attached to the building in front of them—"is the Sixteenth Street Baptist Church."

Scoob nods. The church isn't as big as the one Dad drags him to every Sunday, but a wide set of steps leads to a covered porchlike area set between two square towers with domed roofs. Reminds Scoob of a school. "I see."

G'ma doesn't expound. Which is fine. While, yes, Scoob's wondering if this is another stop she and G'pop never made because of the circumstances, he's not real sure he wants to ask. Cuz, you know: potential G'ma tears and all that.

But then the silence between them stretches on. And on.

Scoob's elbow throbs almost like it's prompting

him to speak up. So he opens his mouth . . . but can't come up with anything to say. So he closes it.

Then G'ma sniffles. Double time: *sniff sniff.*

And there it is.

"Aww, come on, G'ma. Don't cry."

"People can just be so *awful,* Scoob-a-doob," she says.

"Yeah." Bryce's fat head pops into Scoob's brain. "Sucks when they get away with it, too."

"We stopped here." She sniffles again. "Your G'pop and I."

Now she's got Scoob's attention. "You did?"

"Mmhmm. April third, 1968. I'll never forget because it was the day before Martin Luther King Jr. was assassinated. He'd preached in this church. We were halfway through Mississippi the next day when we heard about Dr. King being killed in Memphis."

"Whoa." Scoob knows all about the Reverend Dr. Martin Luther King Jr. He and Dad have gone to Ebenezer Baptist Church and Dr. King's birth home every MLK Day since Scoob learned how to walk. On their most recent visit, Scoob even got on a replica of a segregated bus and sat behind the

"Colored" line. It was . . . well, to be frank, Scoob still hasn't figured out how he *feels* about the whole thing.

"In 1963, this church was bombed by some god-awful men, and four little girls were killed."

"It was *bombed*?" Scoob says.

G'ma nods. "This is where civil rights leaders, Dr. King included, used to gather and strategize.

The same idiots who didn't like seeing your grand-father and me together weren't real keen on black folks having the same rights as white ones. This church stood for something they didn't like, so they tried to blow it up." She shakes her head. "Your G'pop and I were never religious, but we felt we *had* to stop by and pay our respects as we were passing through here on our trip. He stayed in the RV, and I just stood here on the sidewalk like you and I are doing, but seeing the place with our own eyes—"

Speaking of *eyes,* G'ma's narrow, and her sun-shiney old face suddenly reminds Scoob of a rag-ing storm cloud. Like, lightning flashing in it and everything.

"Thirty-nine years," she says. "Took 'em thirty-nine *years* to convict that hateful man who killed those little girls. Can you believe that?"

Scoob's eighty-four percent sure she's not talking to him anymore. But knowing what *he* knows, he can't say he's surprised.

"Meanwhile, they locked my Jimmy up and threw away the key without a second thought. And *he* didn't kill anybody!"

Now Scoob's a *hundred* percent sure she's not

talking to him. Hundred and ten percent, even.

"And I just *let* 'em." G'ma's crying for real now. She wipes her nose on her neon-orange jacket sleeve. "He was a *good* man. And I let him—" More tears streak down, and she shakes her head. "I shouldn't've. It wasn't right. If I could just go back and *fix* it—"

Now she's wringing her hands—which are shaking. It freaks Scoob out a little. Was there something *fixable* about G'pop going to prison?

Why does Scoob feel like there are bugs crawling all over him now?

"Uh, G'ma?" He touches her shoulder, and she jumps. He has to catch her upper arm and waist to keep her from falling. "Whoa. You okay?"

She looks at him like she's seeing a ghost—eyes wide and scared. And she's trembling.

"G'ma?"

She stares at him for a few seconds that feel like *eternities,* then blinks a few times and seems to come back to herself. Her eyebrows tug down, and she slowly pulls her arm away and rights herself. "William? What are you—?" She looks around. "Oh my." Dusts her jogging suit off. "Well, well."

Stands tall. Well, as tall as one can at four eleven. Lifts her chin. "Let's get a move on, shall we?"

"Uhh—"

"Hop to it, kiddo. Need to get across the state line quick as we can. Campsites at the next park are first come, first served."

And she turns on a GOS (*Grandma Orthopedic Sneaker*) and heads back to the RV.

They ride in silence for a good while. Scoob doesn't know what to say, and anyway, his head is spinning, so it's not like he could form sentences if he tried.

Someone tried to blow up a *church* with little kids in it? Also, what did G'ma mean about "fixing" whatever happened with G'pop?

Then there's the whole license plate thing. Scoob looked: there's definitely a Vermont tag on the Winnebago now. Which is strange enough to think about *without* considering G'ma's use of the phrase *make a run for it,* and yet that's dancing around in his mind too.

He sighs and pulls the road map G'ma gave him from his backpack. Opens to the Alabama part and circles Birmingham. Draws a little church over it.

"You making your own annotations over there, kiddo?" G'ma says, breaking the unask-able question spiral Scoob's tumbled into.

"Oh . . . yeah," Scoob says. "Guess I am."

She nods. "Ya know, I'm really glad you're here with me."

He swallows down his unease and forces a smile. "I'm glad I'm here too, G'ma."

Which . . . is partly true? He's definitely glad he's not at home in James Robert Lamar Jr.'s personal version of house arrest. Though he can't help but wonder if G'ma really did send that text message to let Dad know they're okay. Why he's thinking about this *now* he couldn't say, but . . .

He's gotta ask. "G'ma, did you ev—"

"I wanted to take this trip with your daddy," she says.

"You did?" Why he's surprised, he doesn't know. Dad *is* G'ma's son.

"For *years* I wanted to," she says. "But I never did. Never even mentioned it to him."

Hmm. "Why not?"

"Couldn't muster the courage," she says. "Didn't wanna face the questions I knew he'd ask. Especially about your G'pop." She shakes her head.

Now Scoob's uncomfortable again and he's just figured out why: Ever since they were at the church, she's been telling him stuff she normally wouldn't. Almost like they're *friends* instead of grandma and grandkid. It's one thing to talk to somebody *his* age as a friend—he and Shenice obviously talk all the time. But a *grandma*? Grandmas are even more grown-up than regular grown-ups—how's he supposed to even respond?

"Anyway, for a minute at that Yankee restaurant, I felt like *he* was with me. Took me right on back."

Scoob is confused now. "What do you mean, G'ma?"

"The way those people were staring at us? The man with a face the color of a pig's rear end, and the ugly woman with the hooked nose?"

Scoob can't help but smile at her descriptions.

"There was a brief moment when I looked at you and saw your daddy." She turns, and her blue eyes rove over Scoob's face in a way they never have before. "When your daddy was a little boy, and he and I would go different places, people were usually nice to me but crummy to him," she says. "And when they'd find out he was my son . . . well, let's just say I've seen the nice-to-nasty switch flip a few more times than I care to think about.

"There was one time—your daddy was about five, I think. He and I were a few towns away from home because I'd gone to interview for a teaching position at a new school and couldn't find a baby-sitter. Anyway, we go in this grocery store, and Jimmy was upset because I told him he couldn't have a candy or something. Typical kid stuff." She waves her hand like *no big deal*. "He was pulling on my dress and whining a bit, and this store owner comes over with a wooden paddle and says, 'This little n-word bothering you, ma'am? I can take care of 'im. . . .' Except he said *the word*."

Scoob's eyes go wide.

"I'll never forget it. Your daddy was hiding behind my legs, scared outta his wits at that point. When I *kindly* told the man that Jimmy was my son and we were just fine, thank you very much, the old buzzard looked at me like I'd cursed his mama, and kicked us plumb out of the store. Can you believe that?"

"Uhh—"

"I mean, the *nerve* of that man!"

As G'ma seethes, Scoob stares at her little hands on the steering wheel, then down at his own. Where his are the color of a kinda-old penny, hers, though brown-spotted, are so pale he can see the blue of her veins.

And it's not like he never noticed before. It just feels like a bigger big deal than he knew possible. Scoob, after all, is darker-skinned than his dad.

Why does it feel like everything's changing super fast?

"You're an incredible kid, you know that?" G'ma says out of the blue.

"Um . . . thanks, I guess."

"You remind me so much of him."

"Of my dad?" (Which is *not* a compliment as far as Scoob is concerned.)

She shakes her head. "No, no," she says. "Of your G'pop!"

"Oh." The sudden subject switch is disorienting, but Scoob tries to go with it. G'ma's smiling, and yes: it's clear from the past twelve hours there's a lot Scoob doesn't know about his grandfather. But still: the guy spent most of his life in prison. Somewhere Scoob *never* wants to go.

One thing's for sure: no matter how many nice stories G'ma has about James Robert Lamar Sr., Scoob's not so sure being like him in *any* way is a good thing.

Move Forward

Dad calls again—G'ma's phone is actually turned on this time—just as the nice man from the camper parked at the next site over in the Bonita Lakes RV Park finishes connecting G'ma's *sweet ride* to the sewer hookup. Which is perfect timing from every angle: the enchiladas Scoob and G'ma stopped for are ready to make a *swift* exit, and there's no public toilet for him to use. As such, he's able to slip into the Winnebago bathroom as soon as he hears G'ma say, "Yes, Jimmy, we're *fine*. Cool your jets, will ya?"

Scoob tries to tune out, but of course that makes

his hearing sharper. (Funny how that works, isn't it?)

". . . What do you mean is he having any *fun*?"

". . . Oh, now you're just being ridiculous . . ."

". . . No, I do mean that. You're much too hard on the boy."

". . . Fine, fine. You're the father."

". . . Did she now? I'll let him know—oh, I *shouldn't* let him know—?"

And then her voice cuts off as Scoob hears what must be the RV door shutting.

That last part gets his wheels turning. What *she* is G'ma referring to? Shenice? His mom? What does Dad *not* want him to know? Besides *anything* fun or exciting.

His stomach burbles angrily.

By the time he exits the bathroom—after loading it down with "odor-absorbing" air freshener that doesn't seem to be absorbing anything—G'ma's back inside and decked out in her camo gear. "Suit up, kiddo." She tosses Scoob a bundle of . . . he has no idea what.

It does have straps, though. Which he grabs and holds it up.

Camouflage overalls that match hers.

"Well, what are ya waitin' for?" G'ma says. "Hop to it!"

Scoob looks down at his current attire: navy NASA T-shirt, khaki cargo shorts, and sneakers.

"Just switch out of the shorts," she goes on. "I won't look." She turns around.

Scoob can't think of anything to say—or anything *else* to do—so he changes. "Um. I'm done."

"Great!" G'ma says, spinning on the toes of her Velcro shoes with a clap. "Grab your backpack so we can stick my box in it, and let's head out."

Why they need to take the treasure box with them, Scoob isn't sure, but he doesn't bother asking. Also doesn't bother asking what Dad said. G'ma's clearly on a mission.

He does as he's told.

"So . . . where we going?" he asks as they reach the edge of the campground and step onto a trail that leads into some rather *dense*-looking woods. Maybe he should've peeked at the back of the RV to see if she's switched the plates again . . . what if she did and is trying to get rid of the evidence now?

"Oh, just on a little adventure," she says. "You

spend a lot of time handling man-made devices that won't help you in a *true* emergency. I think it's high time you learn some survival skills."

Well, *that* doesn't sound scary at all. . . .

"Your G'ma's gonna teach ya a thing or two, Scoob-a-doob. Come on."

They lapse into silence and walk for a solid fifteen minutes before Scoob realizes he's missing a golden opportunity to get some of his questions asked.

A bird crows overhead like *Go ahead, dummy!* so Scoob clears his throat. "Was that my dad who called?"

G'ma waves a hand as if swatting away a fly. "That old sourpuss. You'd think the man had a very unhappy childhood with the way he behaves sometimes."

"What'd he say?"

"Nothin' important," G'ma replies. She stops to pull something out of her pocket, and Scoob almost smacks right into her.

Up into the air her hand goes, and she rotates this way and that. She's holding a compass. Which, once she picks a final direction, she returns to the pocket, then licks her index finger and puts it just above her head.

Okaaaay . . .

"This way," she says, leaving the trail and heading straight into the forest.

Scoob doesn't move. He looks left and right, up and down. From where he's standing, he can see the sky and a well-trod path that he *knows* will lead him out of these woods no matter which way he follows it. Where G'ma's at, though? The tree canopy is so thick, it basically looks like night in there. That's not to mention all the fallen branches and raised tree roots waiting to trip him. (One still-painful arm gash is enough.)

Or the snakes waiting to bite him.

Or the . . . bears. Waiting to eat him.

"Well, come on, ya diddle-diddle!" G'ma yells

from wherever she is. That camo outfit's working too well for Scoob's liking.

He gulps. "Maybe we should stick to the path, G'ma," he shouts back. *It's here for a reason.*

"Don't be a goose!" she replies. "Better to be in here than out there in the open where the grizzlies can see ya plain as day." Then there's a cackle that echoes so menacingly, Scoob could swear it sends a shudder through the treetops.

He inhales *extra* deep. What the heck was he thinking letting G'ma drag him out into the Mississippi wilderness? This is the same lady who tackled him that one time they were playing baseball in her backyard and he tried to block her from reaching first base!

He takes a step into the woods. "Where even are you, G'ma?" he shouts.

"Follow the sound of my voice," he hears her shout. "That's Survival 101: use your available senses. If you can't see something, you gotta be able to figure out where it is by other means. In this case: use your hearing."

She goes quiet.

"Uhh . . . G'ma?"

Nothing.

Scoob starts to sweat. He knows she's somewhere in front of him, but he wasn't listening carefully enough to tell if she's to the right or to the left. Considering how tightly packed these pines—which look suspiciously like towering dragon-giants in this moment—are, moving even the slightest bit in the wrong direction could be disastrous.

G'ma was probably (*hopefully!*) kidding about the grizzlies, but still: he doesn't want to get eaten.

The trail is right behind him. He could hop onto it and trek right on back to the RV, which, relative to his present surroundings, is the world's lushest palace full of what Dad would call "first-world luxuries." All he'd have to do is shout to let G'ma know he's headed back. Has to pee super bad or something.

Then again, knowing her, she'd tell him to pick a tree.

He'd also be leaving *her* alone out here to be eaten . . .

He's getting a little mad at her now. For putting him in this predica—

"CA-CAAAAW, CA-CAAAAAAAAAW!"

Definitely not a bird, and definitely a bit ahead and to his right.

Scoob steels himself and heads in what he *hopes to the high heavens,* as Dad likes to say when he's being more over the top than usual, is the right direction.

He finds G'ma standing in a small clearing with her veiny little fists on her hips. Just *beaming* like Scoob won an Olympic gold for Not-Dying-in-a-Scary-Forest. Which should definitely be a real sport—it's way harder than running around in a circle. Scoob would know: he went out for track last year.

"Attaboy!" she says.

Scoob rolls an acorn around with the toe of his sneaker. "Thanks, I guess."

"Now come on over here," she says. "It's high time you learn to build a fire."

This is when Scoob actually takes a gander at their surroundings. The open space he and G'ma are standing in appears to be some sort of campsite. There's even a spot smack in the center where a bunch of medium-to-large rocks have been arranged in a haphazard ring. Reminds Scoob of the brick fire pit at the edge of Shenice and Drake's backyard.

"You knew this place was here, G'ma?" Scoob says.

"I did once I found it," she says as she starts walking around the outer edge of the space, peeling off what look like curls of paper from some of the trees as she goes. She also plucks up handfuls of brown grass. "Set your bag down and get to gathering up a bunch of twigs and any dead leaves you see, will ya?"

"Uhh . . . okay."

"And make sure they're dry. You can make a pile right in the center of the fire pit there."

As Scoob sets about his task, his mind returns to all the things he doesn't know but wants to. Like who/what Dad was talking about.

"Keep an eye out for some good sticks and fallen branches, too, Scoob-a-doob. And if you see any good-sized hunks of wood, bring those over as well."

Now Scoob's thinking about Shenice and how this one time, she climbed a huge tree in the woods behind G'ma's house in search of the "perfect jousting stick"—she'd watched some old movie called *A Kid in King Arthur's Court* and become obsessed with "the injustice of the lack of girl knights." Problem was, she got up so high, she freaked. Scoob had to climb up to *be* a prototypical knight and lead her back down. Then literally an hour later in those same woods, Scoob fell into a creek, and she had to save *him*.

Scoob and Shenice always had each other's backs. And fine: Scoob had begun to see her in a different way. Which is why he did what he did when Bryce pushed things too far with Drake and seemed to be threatening her.

Why couldn't Dad understand that?

"How's it going?" G'ma is now bent over the ring of rocks arranging the tree-paper and grass and some of the twigs and leaves Scoob piled in the center. He looks at the handfuls of sticks he's holding. No idea he'd picked up so many.

"Uhh . . . fine, I guess."

"Come on over here. Let's see whatcha got."

Scoob does as he's told, and when G'ma sees what's in his hands, she claps and bounces on her little G'ma toes. "All right, come come. Lemme show you how it's done."

Scoob brings the sticks over, and she makes him squat down to watch as she arranges them into an upside-down cone-type thing (which just makes Scoob want ice cream). There's something about *tinder* and *kindling* and *oxygen,* then she's arranging some bigger hunks of wood that came from who knows where, and pulling a box of super-long matches out of Scoob's bag. How the heck did those even get there?

Sizzle, crackle, pop . . .

And there it is.

A fire.

"Whoa," Scoob says as it catches in earnest.

"Betcha didn't know your G'ma had *them* kinda tricks up her sleeve, didya?" She puts a hand on her lower back and straightens up. Slowly. Reminds

Scoob of her former attic door—had to push it a little harder than all the other ones, and it always groaned as it opened like it was annoyed at being bothered. "Not as nimble as I used to be, but this old bird can still start a darn good fire."

Scoob just stares into the flames. Because learning this new thing about G'ma just makes his head spin around all the *other* new stuff he's learned.

"I tried to teach your daddy how to do this when he was a kid," she goes on, "but he wanted no part of it. Never been the outdoorsy type." She plants her hands on her hips, and now *she's* staring into the flames as though searching for something.

Scoob recognizes the question-asking opportunity. "Was he mad when he called this time?" he asks.

"He's always mad, kiddo."

She can say that again. "But why?"

G'ma just sighs. Which makes Scoob's *Dad* questions bubble up and overflow. "Why's he so hard on me? Why doesn't he listen? Why is nothing I do ever good enough? Why doesn't he understand me? Why won't he give me a break?" Scoob's eyes prickle, but there's no *way* he's gonna cry right now. He grits his teeth to keep the tears in.

G'ma's staring at him now. "Come on over here and have a sit-down," she says. "Actually, help me down first." She stretches her arms out to him.

"You sure about that, G'ma?" What he *doesn't* say is *Are you gonna be able to get up?*

"Yeah, I'm sure." G'ma takes Scoob's hands and slowly lowers herself to the ground. "Now hand me that trinket box from your bag, and then you sit with your back against mine, so we're both supported."

Scoob complies.

Behind him now, he hears the creak of G'ma's treasure box, then she's passing him something over her shoulder. 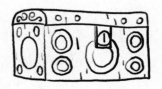 It's a black-and-white photo—in a plastic sleeve—of a white man leaning against a *super*-old-school car with his arms crossed. Scoob turns it over. The back has *Clyde Alexander—1952* written in the top right corner, and what looks like an image of Texas cut from a map. There's a city—Kent—circled in the west of the state, not too far from the Mexico border.

"That's my daddy," G'ma says. "Gave me that

photo right before he hopped in that Chevy and took off. I was nine years old."

Whoa.

"He was my whole world up until that point, so you can imagine how it affected me. I'd overheard him talking about Kent, Texas, so I figured that's where he'd gone—I'm the one who added the cut-out to the back of the photo—but my mama would never confirm or deny it despite my pestering her mercilessly. I knew she knew where he'd run off to and why, but she wouldn't tell me a single thing."

That sure sounds familiar.

"I wouldn't leave well enough alone, though," G'ma continues. "Kept digging and digging until I discovered some things about my daddy I'd've been better off not knowing."

"Like what?"

Scoob feels G'ma sigh against his back. "Well, he wasn't as good a man as I thought, Scoob-a-doob. Did a number of awful things and hurt a lot of people."

"How so?"

"In a word, he was a crook."

"Oh."

"It's possible to know *too* much about the folks in your life. Your daddy's always mad because he knows too much—about your mama, about his daddy . . . at least he *thinks* he knows about his daddy." She sighs again.

"Anyhoo, finding out those things about *my* father at such a young age—well, we'll just say there's a whole lot I wish I could unlearn. It put a lot of mad down inside my belly just like it did your dad."

Which is interesting considering the amount of mad down inside *Scoob's* belly. Is putting mad down inside their kids' bellies just a thing dads do in Scoob's family?

"But you're not like my dad at all, G'ma," he says, grasping at air. "You . . . smile. And laugh."

"Oh, I've let it get the best of me a time or two," she says. "But unlike my daddy, I'm gonna make things right before it's too late."

That gives Scoob pause, and he wants to ask what she means, but before he can, she says, "Let's put out this fire. It's time to move forward."

Onward

At first Scoob thinks he's dreaming.

The trek back to the RV through the woods would've *seemed* uneventful to any casual observer— G'ma babbled about recognizing poisonous plants and berries, Scoob retaining exactly zero of what she said, and also told him Shenice had stopped by looking for him because he hasn't been answering text messages or online gaming requests.

Scoob's mind was elsewhere, though. Between the stuff about G'ma's dad, what it could mean in reference to Scoob's mom, and this whole thing about "making it right," Scoob barely registered eating dinner, getting ready for bed, and climbing up into his over-cab bunk.

In all honesty, the whole random-campfire scenario made him feel like something with G'ma was off. Now, as he hears "I'm gonna fix it!" for the third time and his eyes pop open, he *knows* something is.

"I messed up before. I know it," G'ma mutters at the dark back end of the RV. "I failed you, but I'm making it right. We're going all the way this time, and everything will be fine."

Scoob stares at the ceiling, which seems lower than the previous night, his heartbeat chugging between his ears like a runaway train. He's thirsty. Just like on nights when his brain is too full and he has bad dreams. He always wanders into Dad's room, and the minute he climbs into the king-sized bed, Dad gets up and comes back with a glass of water.

He wishes Dad were here.

Also, his arm hurts. When he went to change the bandage today, the cut was redder than he expected. Seems sorta warm now, but that's probably his imagination.

Anyway, there's no chance he's going back to sleep right now, so he climbs down from the bunk as quietly as possible. He'll play one of those games on her phone where you don't have to think.

He picks it up from the dash and slides into the passenger seat. Presses the unlock button to illuminate the screen.

There are seventeen missed calls. All from Dad.

Scoob punches in the unlock code—his birthdate—and discovers there are also voice mails. He's tempted to listen to one, but if he does, G'ma will know just like Dad must've that time Scoob listened to the message from his mom. He guesses he could just delete it after, since there are seven, it looks like. But that doesn't really sit right either.

Didn't G'ma just talk to Dad earlier? Why would he call so many times if they've already spoken?

G'ma murmurs something incoherent, and then Scoob hears a mechanical creak as she shifts in her bed. He wants to go check on her . . . wake her to let her know Dad's trying to get ahold of them. Because something's not sitting right in the *gut* she's always telling him to trust.

But it's three in the morning. Probably shouldn't wake a sleeping grandma unless there's a tried-and-true emergency. There was one time he screamed bloody murder in her backyard because a bird had pooped on his head, and she came flying out faster than he knew she could run. Said he almost gave her a "gosh-darned heart attack!" Maybe shouldn't do that again.

He sighs. Certainly not in the mind-set to play a game anymore.

Not knowing what else to do, he returns the phone to the dash, then climbs back up into bed. After pulling the bunk curtain shut, he opens the small window near his head and lies faceup. Lets the music of the woods outside—chirping crickets, hooting owls, wind in the leaves—fill his head.

His eyes drift shut.

-- -- -- -- -- -- -- -- --

When Scoob wakes up he's . . . moving?

There's a bump and his entire body lifts from the mattress.

Definitely in motion.

"G'ma?"

"He has risen!" she replies from beneath him.

He shakes his head, though he can't help but grin. "I wasn't dead, G'ma."

"Coulda fooled me . . ."

"What time is it?"

"Eleven forty-three a.m., Central."

Eleven forty-three? Has he really been asleep for eight hours? Scoob flips to his stomach to look out his window. Trees zip by in a blur of bright green.

"Where are we?"

"The grand old city of Meridian!" She breaks out in song: *M, I, crooked letter, crooked letter, I . . .*

This makes Scoob smile. G'ma taught him that when he was maybe three. Took him until second grade to realize he was spelling *Mississippi*.

"There's breakfast down in the fridge for ya, but you might as well hold off since it's darn near lunchtime. We'll stop and stretch our legs. Eat at a real table, and let somebody else do the cookin' and cleanin' for once."

"Okay."

"Why don't you come on down and keep your ol' G'ma company? It's lonely down here without a passenger, Jimmy."

Jimmy.

Which *Jimmy* she's referring to—it's what she

calls Scoob's dad *and* how she sometimes refers to G'pop—Scoob doesn't know. But it makes him uncomfortable either way.

G'ma's moaning and groaning and sleep-talking last night crash over Scoob, and now he *has* to get out of the bunk: it suddenly feels like the ceiling is trying to smush him.

There's no way he can look at her right now, so he grabs his road map for the sake of somewhere to put his eyes just in case. "I'm William, G'ma," he says as he slides into the passenger seat.

"What's that?"

"You called me Jimmy."

"Oh gracious!" She laughs and smacks the steering wheel. "Guess I'm having flashbacks of the *last* time I was in this town!"

That just makes Scoob more anxious. *We're going all the way this time,* she said in her sleep. Going all the way *where*? And why is she so determined to get there now?

Matter of fact, what did G'ma even *see* in G'pop?

"G'ma, what made you marry a criminal?"

"Say *what* now?" Flabbergasted.

"G'pop, I mean," Scoob goes on. "It's just . . .

I know he got sent to prison. What would make a lady like you marry a guy who liked to steal from people?"

"Who says he liked it?"

"Huh?"

"You asked what would make me marry a man who *liked* to steal. What makes you think he liked it?"

Scoob's not sure what to say to that. "I mean . . . he was convicted for a bunch of thefts, right?"

The corner of her mouth twitches. "Yes."

"So?"

G'ma turns to him with her eyes narrowed. Is she . . . mad? Scoob can't remember a single time he's ever made G'ma truly *mad*.

He gulps.

"Let me ask *you* a thing or two," she says.

"Okay . . ."

"Do you like fighting?"

Scoob's jaw clenches. "No ma'am."

"What about computer cheating?"

He sighs. How do grown-ups always manage to flip everything back on the kid? "I didn't cheat, G'ma."

"Allow me to rephrase: Do you like helping others cheat?"

Scoob doesn't reply.

"Well?" G'ma prods.

"No, I don't."

"So people don't have to enjoy the wrong they're doing to do it?"

"I guess not," Scoob says.

"Your grandfather made some poor decisions that hurt people, your father included. But he's not the only one."

Now Scoob's a little mad. "I get it, G'ma. I made some mistakes too—"

"I'm not talking about you, William."

"You're not?"

"No. I'm talking about *me*. I know your dad is still angry with his father. Probably will be for the rest of his life. He's great at holding a grudge, Jimmy Junior is," G'ma says. "But there's a lot he doesn't know."

This makes Scoob *extra* uncomfortable, but what's he supposed to say? "Try telling *him* that."

This makes G'ma laugh. "You've got his wit, for sure."

"Too bad I don't have his 'self-discipline,'" Scoob says with a scowl. "At least that's what *he's* always saying." The words ring through Scoob's head: *You know what you need, William? Some self-discipline. Thought it would run in the blood, but I guess not.* Every time Scoob hears it, he wants to say: *Being criminally minded doesn't run in the blood either. So maybe you could quit treating me like it does.*

By some miracle, he's resisted.

"He'll come around," G'ma says. "You'll see. And if not, who cares? You and me'll be on a beach in Mexico living our best lives."

Scoob's inner alarm bells go off. Now all he's seeing in his head are those seventeen missed calls. He clears his throat. "You . . . uhh . . . talk to him this morning? My dad, I mean."

"Nope," she says. "Haven't heard a word from him since yesterday."

"And he hasn't called?"

"Sure hasn't. Guess he finally decided to take a chill pill." She chuckles.

Speaking of *chill*, Scoob loses the one in his mind and feels a different one shoot down his arms. His eyes dart around the inside of the cabin in search of the phone, but it's nowhere in sight. He knows he didn't erase those missed-call notifications. *Surely* she saw them.

But why would she lie?

She clicks the blinker on to exit the highway, and Scoob gulps. "So where we headed now?"

"Ye Olde Cracker Barrel." They pull to a stop at the top of the exit ramp.

"And then?"

"Then we'll hit a store and restock our supply of vittles and beverages."

"And after that?"

"You sure are full of questions today," she says as she takes a right. She turns to smile at him. It's almost . . . sinister?

Nah. No way.

It's *G'ma,* for goodness' sake.

Pull it together, Scoob.

She faces back forward, but not before Scoob takes note of the (scary?) little spark in her blue eyes. "After that," she says, "onward."

Places to Be

Scoob's apprehension continues through *brunch,* as G'ma calls it. Especially since she makes him bring his backpack inside the restaurant—with her treasure box inside—and glances at it every few minutes like it's going to suddenly sprout legs, hop up, and scurry away.

It's weird.

However, on the way out, when G'ma pulls her phone out of her "pocketbook" to snap a pic of Scoob after making him plop down in one of the wooden rocking chairs on the Cracker Barrel front porch, she discovers it's turned off. How and when it got that way, Scoob doesn't know. He doesn't *think* he shut it off when he was handling it last night, but he guesses it's possible. . . .

Anyway, when she turns it on and says, "Oh, lookie there, your daddy called!" before lifting it to her ear to listen to the voice mails, Scoob's heart unclenches.

So maybe she didn't lie. He takes a huuuuuge breath of Mississippi air into his lungs and blows it out.

Though he still can't help but watch her closely.

Her expression stays neutral, and after half a minute or so, she rolls her eyes and waves her hand in the air like she's swatting away a mosquito and pulls the phone away from her face.

"What'd he say?" Scoob can't help but ask.

"You don't even wanna know. Sit on down so I can get my photo of ya."

Scoob does as she says, and G'ma holds the phone up. Grins. "My most favoritest grandson," she says.

"I'm your only grandson, G'ma."

"Oh hush and bring your heinie," she says with a chuckle before heading back to the Winnebago.

And then just as she said, they head to the grocery store.

On the way back to the highway, though, things take another turn for the strange and unusual. As they're passing a big shopping center, G'ma says, "Ooh, a jewelry store!" and decides to turn off.

"Uhh . . . do we need some jewelry?" Scoob asks.

"Humor me, will ya?"

Not like he has any choice in the matter. She's the adult.

The minute they step inside, G'ma clasps her hands beneath her chin and sighs. You'd think she'd stumbled into heaven.

As she wanders around gazing into the glass cases full of stuff so sparkly, some of it hurts Scoob's eyes to look at, he decides to try and make the most of her distraction.

He sidles up beside her. "So what'd my dad say, G'ma?" he asks all nonchalant-like.

"Oh, you know him," she replies, trying to brush it off.

But Scoob's not letting it slide this time. He *knows* how many times Dad called and how many messages he left. And yeah, the guy can be wound tighter than a spool of thread, but that was a lot even for him. "He want anything in particular?"

"Other than killing all the joy? Nope." She starts whistling.

Which sets Scoob's internal alarms off again. He knows from years of playing Texas Hold'em with G'ma that whistling is her *bluffing* tell.

"You gonna call him back?"

"Ah, maybe later," she says, wandering over to a case at eye level that has a necklace in it with a jewel the size of a Ping-Pong ball. "For now, why don't you tell me more about the latest issue between you two?"

"What do you mean?" Except Scoob has a feeling he knows where this is going.

"I want to hear about the computer cheating," she says.

And just like that, she's flipped it on him again.

Scoob sucks his teeth. "Come on, G'ma," he says, glancing around. The store is empty, but the man behind the central counter with a ring of keys has been watching him since he walked in. He kinda wants to leave. "You don't want to hear that *right now,* do you?"

"Unless you'd rather talk about your young lady friend . . . Shenice?"

"No!" Scoob scratches the back of his neck. *His* nervous tell.

G'ma laughs outright.

"It's just that there are more *interesting* things we could discuss, you know? Like what you were like when you were my age." *Or why we're in a jewelry store.*

When she doesn't respond immediately, Scoob turns to look at her. Her eyes are . . . sad. "Oh, I was a downright *menace* at your age, Scoob-a-doob."

"You *were?*"

"Mmmhmm. I'm not proud of it, but my favorite pastimes at eleven were pickpocketing and petty theft."

Scoob's sure he looks like she just told him she knows Santa's real because they kick it at the North Pole together on weekends. He knows she mentioned some "poor decisions," but . . . *really?* "Whoa."

"This is what I meant earlier. There's a whole *heap* you don't know about your G'ma, kiddo."

Scoob doesn't respond.

"What you *should* know is that I'm concerned. Knowing what I was like at your age, I'm real curious about the *whys* of the trouble you been in." She waves the key-ring man over and points out a ring. It's got red stones running all the way around. She slips it onto a finger and holds her hand up to admire it. "You know, my *name* is Ruby," she says to the guy. *Todd,* his name tag says.

It makes him smile. "It's perfect for you, ma'am," he says.

Now Scoob's smiling too. It really does look pretty good on her.

"So tell me all about this . . . *academic defraudment scandal* is what they called it, right?" she says, jolting Scoob back to the moment.

He rolls his eyes. Mr. Atsbani, the computer science teacher, had been so *extra* about the whole situation. There hadn't been anything "scandalous" about it. "It was all just a big mistake," he says.

"All righty. Do tell."

Scoob sighs. "Everything happened in computer science."

"Mmhmm."

"And like . . . not to brag, but I can do ninety percent of the work in there with my eyes closed and a hand tied behind my back."

G'ma laughs, but Scoob is serious. He's known his way around most computers since pre-k. He *always* got 100 percent on the quizzes Atsbani made them take at the beginning of class every day. Always.

Except for the one time two weeks before spring break when Scoob was going too fast and clicked *B* instead of *C* on question eight.

He remembers smacking his forehead because he'd blurted *"OW!"* in a loud whisper, and a bunch of his classmates had turned to look at him. He was embarrassed about that. But when he finished the quiz and that 90 percent glared tauntingly at him from the score report page?

"I couldn't handle it, G'ma," he says. "All I could hear in my head was Dad's voice rambling on about *careless mistakes* and how they would *ruin my future.*" He shakes his head. "I considered going to my teacher—"

"Was it really that big a deal, though, kiddo? You said you'd gotten all one hundreds prior . . . what's one ninety?"

"Well—" But how can he explain? The way Dad puts it, there will always be people who don't want to see boys like Scoob do well (Dad's never said it explicitly, but Scoob knows he means *black* boys), so it's vital that Scoob never give anyone a reason to doubt his capabilities. Which is something Scoob understands beneath his skin and down in his bones somewhere but doesn't know how to put into words. "I mean, Dad says—"

"Oh, fiddlesticks on that," she interrupts, which

so surprises Scoob, he jumps. "That old goat. Go on with your story."

"Uhh . . . okay . . ."

"Sorry," she says. "He's just always been so hard on himself, your dad has, and it grinds my gears that he's transferring it to you." She waves to Todd again. Points out a pair of earrings Scoob *thinks* are diamond, though they have a pinkish tint.

"Ah, *yes,* the fancy intense pinks!" Todd crows as he hands them to her. "Excellent choice!" He lays a mirror on the counter.

"What happened next with your teacher?" she asks Scoob as she sticks the skinny posts into her wrinkly earlobes.

Scoob sighs, trying to re-center himself in the story. "It's not that I thought the teacher would change my grade or anything. I just wanted him to know I *knew* the right answer. But when I looked up he was, like . . . laser-eyeing me like I'd farted in class or something."

G'ma lets out a barking "HA!"

Scoob smiles and continues. "Dad would say I'm 'making excuses,' but I really don't think Mr. Atsbani likes me very much. Every time I get a good grade or raise my hand to answer one of his questions, he frowns. Anyway, deep down, I knew I'd have to cut my losses and take the L—"

"The L?"

"For *loss.*"

"Ah, I see. Go on."

"But it was bugging me *so bad* that I knew the right answer but accidentally got it wrong."

"So what happened next?" she asks.

"Well, there were still eight minutes left on the quiz clock, so I decided to use the extra time to take a peek at the coding," he says. "The quizzes are always multiple choice, and the way the software was set up, choosing an answer on a question takes you straight to the next question. So I was *trying* to see if there was a way to change an answer from the inside."

"Mmhmmmm . . ." G'ma points to a necklace with a ruby pendant and a bracelet covered in diamonds shaped like . . . diamonds. "Last two, I promise," she tells Todd with her crinkly smile as he unlocks another case.

"Whatever you need, ma'am. And take your time. I'm here all day." *Wink.*

As soon as he walks away, Scoob goes on. "I swear I wasn't going to change it, G'ma. I just wanted to see if it was possible."

"Okay. And?"

"Well, once I skimmed the block of code, I saw where I could change the score my teacher would see on my computer screen when he walked around the room to jot down everybody's grades. So I gave it a try. I knew from seeing the rest that all I'd have to do to get my *actual* score to reappear was click the refresh button."

G'ma steps up to the big mirror and examines

her newly bedazzled self. "You're speakin' Greek now, but continue." She turns this way and that.

Scoob sighs. "What I'm saying is there was a spot on the back end where I could change *ninety* to *one hundred,* and when I did, and then returned to the score report screen, it read *one hundred percent.*"

"William!" G'ma puts one little fist on her hip all indignant-like.

"I didn't *leave* it that way, G'ma." (Though he'd definitely wanted to.) "Like I said, when I refreshed the page, my real score came back."

Which is where the trouble began. For one, when Atsbani came around to record scores and got to Scoob's, he made some snide remark about how Scoob's "boastful lack of attention during class" was "finally making its mark." That made Scoob angry—and made Dad's words about people not *wanting* Scoob to do well that much more real.

Scoob was so mad, in fact, that when, for two, Cody Williams, the soccer superstar who sat to Scoob's left—and constantly "stretched" so he could get a peek at Scoob's screen during class—approached Scoob and said he'd seen what Scoob had done with the scores and wanted to learn how to do it?

Well . . . Scoob agreed.

And Cody was careful: he changed his scores gradually over the next few days and told Atsbani he'd been studying harder.

Did Scoob feel a pang of guilt every time he heard Cody clicking around to change his score? Yeah, he did. But Scoob ignored it.

He wasn't the one cheating, after all.

Except then things got complicated: Because Cody taught Dasia. And Dasia taught Holly. And Holly taught Bryce. And on. And on. Within a couple weeks, the class quiz average had risen to 97 percent.

And Atsbani got suspicious.

"I'll never forget the day everything came crashing down," Scoob says as they approach the center counter and G'ma begins to remove all the jewelry she's wearing. "I could *see* it coming. Atsbani started his score-marking stroll like usual, but when he got to Bryce's computer, he stopped. When his beady eyes got all squinty and he turned to look back at the computers he'd already checked, I knew it was over."

"Well, that sure sounds bleak." G'ma takes the earrings off one by one and sets them down.

"It was dead silent," Scoob continues. "Atsbani reached out and pushed a key on Bryce's keyboard, went 'Mmhmm,' and then made us all get up and go stand at the back of the room. I knew he was pressing F5 at each computer before writing scores down."

"F5?" G'ma asks.

"Yeah. *Refresh*."

After Atsbani wrote the *real* scores down, he told everyone to stay put, then left the room. Not a single person breathed a word in his absence. He returned four minutes later with the principal in tow. "What's nuts is that despite the fact that *my* score was one of four that didn't change, Bryce ratted me out as the mastermind."

"Yowza." From G'ma.

"Yeah. Atsbani wanted me *'expelled with utmost celerity!'* but Dad and Principal Armand settled on a five-day suspension."

Bye-bye, spring break.

Bye-bye, freedom.

He sighs.

Todd approaches again. "So whattya think, young lady?" he says to G'ma. "Anything tickle your fancy?"

"Oh, I can't afford any of this," she says, unlatching the necklace and laying it down all nice. Then the bracelet. "Though I appreciate you letting an old gal dream big for a bit. When you get to be my age, ya never know when you'll just—" She makes a choking sound and drags an index finger across her neck.

Todd's eyes go wide. Scoob's do too.

"Uhh . . . G'ma?"

"All righty then," Todd says, sweeping the jewelry from the counter and clearly as uncomfortable with G'ma's declaration as Scoob is. "You-all enjoy your Sunday." And he jets off.

When they get to the door and G'ma goes to push it open, Scoob notices a flash of red on her hand. "G'ma, wait!" he says. "You forgot to take the ring off!"

That gets Todd's attention.

Oddly enough, G'ma looks more caught than shocked. Her face is as red as a raspberry. "Oh my!" she says. *Over*-says. Honestly, she looks the same way Bryce did the one time a teacher saw him shove Drake in the school hallway. He tried to play it off and said he'd tripped.

What the heck is going on?

"Welp. Guess that's the end of fantasy jewelry shopping for *this* old bird! I'm clearly losing my marbles!"

Todd slowly outstretches his hand as G'ma crosses the store, and Scoob can see he ain't exactly buying her story.

But he does let them leave.

"Well, that was a close one!" G'ma says as they head back to the RV. Which is when Scoob notices the license plate. Which is white again . . .

But says Tennessee.

"Let's get a move on," G'ma says as if the previous fifteen minutes never happened. "We got places to be."

Stays In

Scoob's so baffled—by everything—that when G'ma tries to continue the jewelry store conversation (like she didn't just try to steal from it?), he rolls with it.

"So why'd you do it?" she says. "Help people cheat."

In truth, Scoob's been so indignant over the fact that he was the only person to get in trouble despite *not* actually cheating, he hasn't given this part much thought. Why *did* he show Cody how to change the score? It's not like Scoob didn't know exactly what Cody was planning to do.

But could Scoob have said no? He guesses he

could've technically, but Cody is one of the most popular guys in school. Scoob has to admit he enjoyed all the smiles and head nods and fist bumps he got from his classmates during those two weeks. He felt . . . *cool*. Appreciated.

Something he certainly didn't feel at home . . .

"I mean, it was nice feeling like people *liked* me again," he says. "After that fight with Bryce, it's almost everybody was scared to get too close. Like they thought I'd go all Bruce Leroy on someone at any moment."

G'ma's bark laugh fills the RV, and Scoob smiles. She's the one who introduced him to the African American karate master. Though he has to admit the movies were kinda over the top.

"Wild, ain't it?" she says, seeming suddenly sadder.

"Huh?"

"How easy it can be to do the wrong thing."

Scoob doesn't respond to that, and she doesn't say anything more.

He does, however, decide to pipe up when, at the next traffic light, she hangs a right instead of a left. "Not to question your sense of direction, G'ma, but shouldn't we be going the other way? I think the highway's behind us."

To Scoob's surprise, G'ma sighs more heavily than he's ever heard her sigh before, and when she turns to him, her eyes are all mopey and full of sadness.

Which makes Scoob feel terrible. "Umm . . . I mean—" His throat gets tight and he looks out the window.

"I just miss him, Scoob-a-doob," G'ma says with a creak in her voice like the rusted hinge of the old toolshed in her backyard he was never supposed to play in but did all the time. "I miss him so darn much, and there's so many things I didn't do right." She eases to a stop at a red light and rotates her cotton-topped head in Scoob's direction. "Think you can indulge your old G'ma in a little nostalgia?"

At the look on her face, all "destitute," as Shenice would say in her *grown woman* voice (he's really starting to miss her), Scoob feels like cracks are forming all over him and he's gonna break into a jillion and one pieces like a smashed Lego tower. He feels like all the rules are flip-flopping just like they did last night when G'ma was talking in her sleep: he's the grown-up now, and she's a little kid needing "a safe space to be sad"—something she used to insist *he* needed.

It's also strange hearing her ask his permission.

"Of course, G'ma. We can go wherever you want."

She nods just as the light changes, and within a few minutes, they're creeping at a snail's pace down a street lined with mostly boarded-up buildings. Reminds Scoob of something out of one of the forbidden-to-them horror flicks he, Shenice, and Drake used to watch on the iPad after the adults went to bed.

He'd wind up sleeping in Dad's bed for three nights after.

As he looks around him now, Scoob's mouth goes dry and he gets a shiver down both his arms. He kinda wishes Dad were here. "Uhh, G'ma?"

It's like she doesn't hear him. "I can't believe it," she whispers. "It's all gone. All of it."

They continue down the road—Fifth Street, Scoob notes as they pass a sign—then G'ma pulls into a parallel-parking spot. Once the RV is shut off, she covers her face with both hands and begins to quietly weep.

Scoob has no earthly idea what he's supposed to do. All he knows is her grandma whimpers feel like stabs straight to the heart—and as much as he hates himself for it, Scoob starts to feel mad at her.

For not telling him where they are or where they're going. For bringing him here to this weird ghost town place with no explanation. For breaking down this way and putting him in this uncomfortable position.

"I'm sorry, Scoob-a-doob," she says as if she can hear his thinking. Which makes him feel even worse. "This place—this *street* . . ."

She crumples into whimpery sobs again.

Scoob closes his eyes and takes one of the deep breaths Drake sometimes has to take when there's too much going on and he gets overwhelmed. Then he grabs the box of Kleenex, reaches across the space between the seats, and puts a hand on G'ma's back.

"G'ma, it's gonna be okay," he says. "*We're* gonna be okay."

She pulls a couple tissues, blows her nose like an elephant, then puts her baby-blue eyes on his brown ones. Her chin is still quivering, but she smiles. "You're such a good egg, Jimmy. I'm the luckiest woman alive."

Scoob gulps, and that *nervous* rock reappears in his gut, tripled in size. "I'm William, G'ma. Scoob."

She turns to look at him and squints for a sec. "Of course you are," she says.

"You . . . called me Jimmy again."

"I did?"

"Mmhmm."

"Oh." Her gaze drifts out the window, and they lapse back into that stuffy silence that makes Scoob itchy all over. Definitely nothing for *him* to say now.

After a minute or so, he hears her sigh and say, "All right, Ruby Jean. Pull it together. Grab ahold of these granny panties and buck on up, now."

At this, Scoob chuckles. "Gross, G'ma."

"You hush," she says, removing her seat belt and rotating her seat all the way around so it's facing the live-in part of the RV.

"Whoa," Scoob says.

"Didn't realize we could do that, huh? I'm gonna

pop into the little girls' room for just a moment, get back to myself. Then I'll tell ya where we are, and we'll press on." She rocks a couple times in the seat, then pushes up to her full stature. Much more adorable than imposing, Scoob notes.

The moment the bathroom door clicks closed, G'ma's cell starts blaring from one of the cup holders, and a scowling face appears on the screen.

Dad.

Scoob freezes, heart thumping so fast in his ears, it practically drowns out the sound of the phone.

Should he answer it? What would he even say? Not five minutes ago, Scoob *wanted* Dad, but now that he's calling . . . what if Scoob answers and Dad starts going off the way he does?

The ringing stops, and Scoob exhales—

But then it starts up again.

"Who's that?" G'ma says, materializing, it seems, at Scoob's shoulder and reaching for the vibrating device. She startles him so bad, *he* instantly needs to go to the bathroom. The phone stops ringing as she brings it closer to her face to read the caller ID.

Then immediately starts again.

"Oh, that old sourpuss," she says. The phone

goes silent, but Scoob has a hunch it's just gonna ring again.

"Maybe you should answer," he says, hardly believing the words are leaving his mouth. "That's the third time he's called in a row." And then there's all those times he called yesterday. Why is G'ma acting so funny when it comes to Dad? And why's Scoob going all sweaty in the armpits?

"So he can poo on our party?" G'ma says. "Nuh-uh." She shakes her head. "Nohow, no way, no sir. We're on a *mission,* Scoob-a-doob."

Scoob feels like his heart is getting bigger with each beat and will eventually explode from his chest as he watches her gnarled index finger hold the button on the side of the phone to shut it all the way off. She returns it to the cup holder.

"I gotta pee," he blurts.

"Well, get a move on, Silly Billy!" G'ma checks her watch, then pulls the treasure box from his bag and sets it on the dining booth table. Lifts the lid and reaches into her pocket. Looks up at him. "Well, whatcha waiting for?"

"Oh." As he scrambles up from his seat, she pulls a gold necklace with a small pendant from somewhere within the depths of the lacquered box and lays it neatly to the side. As Scoob passes, a pair of diamond earrings appear on the table as well.

Pinkish ones.

Eerily similar to the ones he last saw on the jewelry store counter after G'ma removed them from her ears.

It's nothing short of a miracle that the pee actually stays in.

A (Not) Good Feeling

While Scoob's in the bathroom, it occurs to him how odd it is that G'ma just *went* into his bag without permission. That's . . . unlike her.

Yes, it's her treasure box and she can do as she pleases with it, but G'ma's usually all about respecting Scoob's "agency." In fact, her house was the one place where he was allowed to close his door. He knows it shouldn't be a big deal, but this just feels like another brick added to the pile of changes he feels he'll eventually be crushed beneath. In this moment, he misses his old life. He's only been gone a couple days, but he'd give anything to catch a whiff of the flowery perfume Shenice started wearing at the beginning of the year, or hear one of Drake's corny jokes. He even misses Dad's rumbly laugh—which he hasn't heard very often in the past few months, but still.

Why does everything feel so *off*?

"I wanna show you one more thing before we get back on the road," G'ma says, snatching Scoob out of his thoughts (which may not be such a bad thing). She spins on her sneaks and takes the three steps to the door with something green clutched in her hand.

Scoob is frozen to the spot.

Which G'ma seems to sense. As she shoves the door open, she turns to him. "Well? Ya coming?"

Scoob breathes in suuuuuuper deep through his nose. Blows it out of puckered lips. The Green Book wasn't even in his backpack; it was under the pillow in his bunk. Which would mean she poked around up there without his permission as well.

He doesn't know *what* to think or feel now. Technically it's *her* pillow in *her* bunk because this is *her* Winnebago. It's also *her* Green Book.

But . . .

Scoob shakes his head and forces his feet to move. "Yeah. I'm coming."

– – – – – – – – –

Once they touch down on the sidewalk and the RV door clicks closed, G'ma's the speechless one. She looks at the stuff in her hand and instantly appears on the verge of tears again.

Scoob wonders if it's a good idea for them to see what she wants to show him. "You know, G'ma, if this is too painful for you, we can just go," he says with maybe too much hope in his voice.

If G'ma picks up on it, she doesn't let it show. "No, no," she says. "It's important for both of us. Come on."

They head back away from the RV. It's strange: the sidewalks look brand-new, and the redbrick street makes him wonder if the road will lead him to a wizard who can send him back home. The one in *The Wiz* is yellow, but same concept, right?

However, most of the buildings they pass aren't only boarded up: they're beyond hope of repair.

There are even a few gaps *between* dilapidated buildings where Scoob can tell there used to be . . . well, more building.

They stop at the intersection of Fifth Street and Twenty-Fifth Avenue, and she stares across the street at a rusted corner marquee as she hands him the Green Book. His eyes rove the cover again and stick on *1963*. What must a street like this have looked like way back *then*?

"Go to the Mississippi section and find Meridian," she says. "Page thirty-three, second-to-last listing."

Scoob looks at the line—which is underlined— then up at the marquee. Both say *Hotel E. F. Young Jr.*

"Whoa" is all Scoob can think to say.

Then G'ma passes him something else. "Have a look-see."

A photo.

Of G'pop. Standing beneath the marquee. Scoob holds it up to eye level, shifting his focus between the hotel in the

picture and what's right in front of him. "Double whoa," he says.

"That's the last picture I ever took of your G'pop, and the last good night he and I ever had together was inside of that hotel," G'ma says. "Believe it or not, this place used to be mighty fine. There was a barbershop and beauty salon and a shoeshine place all inside. They say Dr. King even stayed here once. It was glorious."

Scoob glances in her direction and isn't surprised to see tears weaving down over her wrinkly cheeks.

"I wish I had the words to express how *hard* it was for your grandfather and me to be a couple, Scoob-a-doob," she says. "Frankly, black folks weren't any keener on it than white folks were. Part of the reason we got the RV is so we wouldn't have to worry about a place to sleep while on the road. The woman working the front desk at *this* place didn't even want to book us a room."

"Really?" Scoob says.

"Really. Manager happened to pass by while she was giving us trouble. I wasn't feeling too hot at that point—it was during our stay here that I first realized we probably weren't gonna make it much further on our trip—and I think he could tell we needed the kindness."

"What was wrong with you?" Scoob asks.

G'ma shakes her head. Sighs. "We'll get there, Scoob-a-doob. We'll get there."

And she turns to head back to the RV.

Scoob *might've* made it back to center—more concerned with G'ma's sadness than his own unease—if he hadn't caught sight of the Tennessee license plate on the rear bumper of the RV again.

This time, the uneasiness is impossible to shake. Even once they're inside and their seat belts are fastened and the engine is cranked. Even when G'ma says, "Scoob-a-doob, not to get all sappy on ya, but it means the world to me that we made this pit stop. It's like closing a door almost."

Scoob gives a vague nod and grunt and bites his thumbnail. Wishes he'd thought to grab his map so he could add a drawing of the marquee over *Meridian* just for something to do.

She keeps going. "Last time I was here was the beginning of the end of a journey, but this time feels like the end of the beginning. You know what I mean?"

"Mmm . . . not really," he says, too mentally exhausted to lie.

"That's all right." She nods. "You'll understand soon enough."

What the heck is that *supposed to mean?*

"We're gonna make it this time, Scoob-a-doob," G'ma continues. "All the way to Juárez. It's what your G'pop would want. I just know it."

Scoob squints. Remembers the Green Book he's still holding and the fact that there's an international section in the back. He saw it while flipping through in Alabama night before last.

Tourist Camp—Jardín Fronterizo is circled in the Mexico section on page eighty. "You'll help me, right?" She glances at him briefly just as the traffic light they're approaching goes green. Which feels all the way wrong considering how much Scoob wants to *stop*. "If something happens and I need your help, you'll do as I say and you'll help me, right, kiddo?"

Scoob gulps. Tries to swallow down the words he *doesn't* want to say forming in his throat.

But it's no use. She's his G'ma. "Of course I'll

help you," he says, doing the *exact* thing that got him wrangled into the cheating scandal.

"Good," she says. "Cuz I've got a good feelin'."

All Scoob can do is sigh. Why's it so hard to just say no when *he's* got a *not*-good feeling?

Off the Grid

But this time, after just a few minutes, Scoob can't take it anymore. "G'ma, was this house-on-wheels made in Tennessee?" he says without looking in her direction.

She turns the radio down. "What's that?"

"I noticed we have a Tennessee tag," he continues. "So I was wondering if the Winnebago company is based in Tennessee or something." He faces his window and clenches his jaw.

Not the least bit smooth.

And G'ma doesn't reply.

Now what's he supposed to say?

His eyes shift and latch on to her powered-down cell. "You mind if I use your phone?"

"Depends on who you wanna call," and she winks.

Probably shouldn't call Dad, then. She'll be able to see it on the call log and might get mad or something. And who knows what she'll do *then*? "Just wanna holler at Shenice. See what she's up to."

"Shenice, huh?"

"Yeah."

No response.

"I kinda miss her," he adds, upping the mushy factor. Grandmas can't resist that, right?

She pulls her focus from the road to look at him . . . suspiciously?

Then she smiles. "That'll be fine."

With relief tingling at his fingertips, Scoob grabs the thing and unbuckles his seat belt.

"Where ya goin'?" she says.

"Oh. I could use a little privacy, if you don't mind."

She shakes her head. Which makes Scoob feel like a helium balloon is expanding in his throat. He knows if he tries to respond, either his voice will crack, or all that'll come out is a squeak.

"No can do, kiddo," she says. "Not safe for you to walk around back there while we're in motion. You wanna call Shenice, gotta do it right where you're sitting. With your seat belt fastened."

"Oh." Scoob *could* bring up all the times he's already walked around "back there" while they're in motion (he very specifically recalls being asked to grab a Grandma Protein Shake not too long after they began their journey), but he doesn't want to push it.

Guess he *won't* be telling Shenice about everything going on and how weird and uncomfortable it makes him feel. But he certainly can't *not* make the phone call now.

He makes sure the ringer switch on the side is set to silent before hitting the power button. Doesn't want her snatching it from his hand if the message notification happens to chime—

And it's a good thing he does because there are three *new* voice mails.

All from Dad.

Scoob knows it's a risk, but instead of actually calling Shenice, he makes a show of dialing the number—in case G'ma is sneaking glances in his direction—then taps to switch over and listen to a voice message instead.

He puts the phone to his ear and smiles at G'ma, feeling "guilty as sin," as she would say. Then Dad's voice comes pouring out of the ear speaker:

> Mama, I don't know where you and William are or why you're not answering my calls or if you even still *have* this phone, but I . . . I need you to call me back. Immediately. Some . . . *authorities* came by here and they're saying you . . . Mama, I need you to call me back. Now. Please.
> **click**

For a second, Scoob sits frozen, the phone attached to his face as if glued there. He blinks. And blinks.

"You all right over there, Jimmy?" comes G'ma's voice, slicing through the block of ice Scoob feels trapped in.

"Yeah," he says. "Umm. Shenice isn't answering. I'm gonna leave a voi—" But he catches himself because if he says *voice mail*, it might tip her off. He quickly pulls the phone down and taps to delete the message he just listened to. "I'll try her again later," he says.

"All righty."

"And umm . . . I'm William, G'ma."

"Mmhmm, sure are," G'ma replies. And she holds out her hand for the phone.

Scoob takes what he hopes is a not-obvious deep breath. He knows what he needs to do and that it's now or never. "You mind if I call my dad too, G'ma? I'd like to check in with him. Make sure he's doing okay at home without me and all that."

"Maybe later," she says. "You know how he is. Can't have him spoiling our good time, now can we?"

Scoob grips the phone a little tighter. "Guess not."

"Now hand it over."

Except now he's got a *real* a problem. Because if she were to check the call log right, it would be clear that Scoob lied to her: he never actually placed the call to Shenice's number.

So as much as he wants to leave it on so he can snatch it up and answer the next time Dad calls—

why isn't he calling *now?*—Scoob shuts the thing off.

Then he lays it against her outstretched palm.

When she pushes the button that usually makes the screen light up and nothing happens, her eyes narrow just the teeniest bit. "You turned it off?"

Scoob can hardly breathe now. "Yeah. It was off when I picked it up, so I figured—"

He doesn't have a clue how to finish that sentence.

Which turns out to be fine. After a second, G'ma nods. "Good," she says. She drops the phone into the small storage space on the driver's-side door where Scoob can't reach it. "You and I are going *off the grid.*"

A Bad Omen

Scoob spends the next hour and a half doodling in the margins of his map while G'ma's favorite band, Earth, Wind & Fire, croons them into the unknown (for Scoob at least). Then G'ma signals to exit the interstate again. "One more drive-by pit stop, then on to Vicksburg for refreshments," she says.

Scoob just sighs and puts a little star over Vicksburg as they ease to a stop at the top of the exit ramp.

"This time I think I'll tell ya where we're headed," she continues, lowering the volume of "Boogie Wonderland." The song always makes him think of penguins; the waddly cold-weather creatures sang and danced to it in one of Scoob's favorite movies.

"I don't think we'll get out once we get there cuz we need to mosey on," G'ma continues, "but I know if we drove through Jackson without me finally seeing this place, I'd regret it forever."

"Is that where we are?" Scoob replies, spotting it on his map.

"Mmhmm. Good ol' Jackson, Mississippi. Your G'pop and I attempted to take this detour fifty-one gosh-darn years ago. Can you believe that?"

Scoob can't, but he doesn't say so.

"There was a man back then: Medgar Wiley Evers. Fought for this country in World War Two, then came home to fight for Negro rights. Real good fella," she says.

"Now I'll be honest with ya, Scoob-a-doob: your ol' G'ma had her head in the clouds when your G'pop and I attempted this trip. We began our courtship in 1961 but were together six years before we tied the knot because it wasn't *legal* for whites and blacks to marry until sixty-seven.

"There was a couple in Virginia who'd been convicted of a *crime* for marrying, and your G'pop

wasn't willing to take the risk of marrying in secret," she says. "But when the Supreme Court over-
turned those dumb laws across the nation? Don't
think I'd ever been so happy."

Scoob grins.

"Not everyone was, though." She hangs a right
into a neighborhood and then follows a short curve
around to a street on the left. "Your G'pop and I
tied the knot at a courthouse, and the civil rights
movement was gaining momentum, but racial ten-
sions were *high*—"

And she stops.

Driving *and* talking.

Scoob follows her gaze to the house across the street. Parts of it are painted a blinding turquoise color, and there's a plaque on the brick part, but he can't see from this distance. Looks like there's also a plaque in the front yard.

G'ma hasn't said a word. Or moved. She's just . . . staring.

That's when Scoob notices something's *off* about the structure itself. He looks at the house next door, and then at the one whose curb they're idling beside.

It hits him.

"There's no front door," he says.

"Entrance is in the carport," G'ma murmurs without pulling her eyes away.

"Oh." Weird.

"Had it built that way cuz they thought it'd be safer," she says.

"Who thought it'd be safer? And safer for what?"

"Safer for the family," she says. "This was Medgar Evers's home, Scoob-a-doob. The man I mentioned."

"Oh. Okay," Scoob says. Is he supposed to say more?

"I can't believe—"

Scoob waits for her to go on.

"I don't know what to say," she says.

Apparently Scoob doesn't either.

"Go in my box—it's in the cabinet above the kitchenette sink—and hand me the . . . radio that's in there."

"Okay." Scoob gets out of his seat to do as she asked. Though what G'ma could need an old *radio* for, he's not sure. There's no way the thing actually works.

He's quick to hand it over when he gets back to the cab, though, because what little color G'ma had has disappeared from her face like she's seeing something Scoob can't at the house-with-no-front-door.

A ghost?

"G'ma, are you okay?"

She doesn't answer. Just unscrews what Scoob *assumed* was an antenna to reveal a clear spout . . . which she then puts to her mouth before turning the "radio" upside down.

To drink from it.

"Whew," she says after a good few gulps. She

squeezes her eyes shut and her head and shoulders quiver. "Forgot how much that burns."

Burns? Scoob's known G'ma going on twelve years and has *never* seen her drink anything other than water and unsweet tea with a quarter of a lemon squeezed over the top. There's no way she's drinking—

"G'ma, is that *alcohol*?"

"Bourbon. It was your G'pop's favorite."

Scoob's dumbfounded.

"And this was his flask," she continues, holding up the radio.

"Wait—" But Scoob's got so many questions, he's not sure which one to ask first. *What's a "flask"? Why's that one shaped like a radio? Since when does G'ma drink?*

The thing he says: "What you just drank was fifty years old?"

She bursts out laughing. And doesn't stop.

For like two minutes. Solid. Scoob literally watches the clock.

At least the color returns to her face, though. The tears leaking from her eyes are running down *very* pink cheeks now.

She eventually takes a breath. "Good lord. Haven't laughed like that in years. And boy, did I need it."

Scoob exhales. He doesn't know how much more of this he can take.

"Thank you, Jimmy. Thank for being here and being YOU."

"I'm *William*, G'ma," Scoob mumbles.

"I just can't believe we're *here*. That *I'm* here. The house is *right there*." She shakes her head again. "After all these years."

And now Scoob really can't take any more. "G'ma, I don't mean to be rude, but where is *here*? And what is that house? And why are *we* here? Now. In front of it."

"That house is a piece of history, Scoob-a-doob."

So she *does* remember who he is.

"It was built to house Medgar Evers's family. Medgar was known for helping black folks get registered to vote back in the day. Also drew national attention to the horrible crime committed against the Till boy. Emmett. *He* was killed just a few hours north of here."

Now she's got Scoob's attention. He knows all

about Emmett Till because Dad gave him a lecture after the *academic defraudment scandal:* said as a black boy, even if Scoob claims he's not doing anything wrong, the moment someone white *says* he is, he's in trouble. He used Emmett Till as an example, and despite the fact that it happened so long ago, the story shook Scoob down to his bones. Especially when Dad told him Emmett really *hadn't* done anything wrong, and the men who did the true wrongdoing—his killers—got off scot-free.

"Medgar was shot down dead right there in the driveway," G'ma says, shoving Scoob out of his musings with so much force, his head swims.

"HUH?"

"House has no front door because the family thought it'd be safer if the entrance was in the carport. But even that didn't protect Medgar. He was shot as he got out of his damn car."

"Wow . . ."

"And it took thirty years for the man who did it to see any jail time."

Scoob is speechless.

"I wanted to come here before," G'ma continues. "I knew we'd be passing through. Had it circled on my map before we started the trip. Jimmy and I were together when we heard about Medgar's murder, and it hit me how much danger your G'pop was in by existing. It's the moment I knew I wanted to marry him."

Scoob just shakes his head. He feels like he's getting punched from multiple angles and can't figure out where to block.

Then her chin gets to trembling.

"It was all my fault," she says as the tears begin to roll. She stretches the alcoholic radio out and he takes it. Shoves it in the glove box.

She keeps going. "I was driving and determined to have my way, even though Jimmy said coming by here'd be a bad omen. He'd fallen asleep, so I went ahead and took the exit. Didn't get a quarter mile before a highway patrol car pulled me over." She shakes her head.

"I remember like it was yesterday: Jimmy piped up to ask why we were stopping, and I yelled at him to hush and stay hidden. I *knew* if those officers saw him with me, they'd come up with a reason to cart him off to jail. The sun was starting to dip in the sky, and I'll never forget it because as the officers stepped up to the RV—there was one on each side—I wondered if it was the last sunset I'd ever see with your G'pop."

Scoob swallows hard. "Was this a Sundown Town?" He'd seen the term in the Green Book and knew it referred to places where black people could be killed just for being there after dark, and no one would bat an eyelash.

"I'm not entirely sure. But it's likely."

"Man, I hate this world sometimes." It's his first time ever expressing it aloud.

"Me too, Scoob-a-doob. Those officers started asking questions, and I could tell they were suspicious. Jimmy wasn't the only contraband I had on board."

Contraband?

"They let me—*us*—go, but I was real shaken up. To this day, I feel like all the terrible stuff that came after was because of me. If I hadn't taken that exit, we'd've never gotten pulled over, and I wouldn't've been in such a terrible state. We wouldn't've had to turn around. I'd've been *fine,* Jimmy. We'd've *made* it."

Scoob's too nervous to correct her this time.

He does think they should get away from here, though.

"We should really go, G'ma," he says. His eyes latch on to the glove box, where the "radio" is sitting like a bourbon-filled brick. Stuff doesn't even *sound* tasty. "Are you . . . okay to drive?" Because he obviously can't.

She stares at the Evers house. Scoob's not even sure she heard him.

"G'ma?"

"Fine, fine, we're going." She puts the RV in gear, and it jerks forward, making Scoob's stomach somersault up into his throat. Between everything she told him and her white knuckles on the wheel, Scoob wonders if G'pop was right: maybe coming here *was* a bad omen.

THE PELICAN STATE

STATE MOTTO

"Union, justice, and confidence."

STATE TREE
Bald cypress

STATE BIRD
Brown pelican

☆ BATON ROUGE

LOUISIANA

STATE FLOWER
Magnolia

FUN FACT
"YOU ARE MY SUNSHINE"
IS THE STATE SONG.

So Far from Home

They ride in silence for a short while—no music even—but when G'ma spots the exit sign for Edwards, MS, she gasps. They don't *take* the exit, thank goodness, but as soon as they pass beneath the bridge, G'ma bites her lip. "Apologies, William, but I have to pull over."

Scoob doesn't move a muscle as they glide to a bumpy stop on the "shoulder" of the highway, or so Dad calls it. He *truly* wishes Dad were here now. This whole day has been a lot, and even Dad's signature scowl would make Scoob feel more stable.

"I know I said we were gonna keep it moving, but

that exit we just passed . . ." She faces him. "That city was our stopping point last time. It's where we turned around."

Scoob's not sure what he expected her to tell him, but it wasn't *that*. Nice to know he's finally gonna get an answer to *one* of his questions: "Why *did* you turn around, G'ma?"

"Your father."

"My father?"

"Yep."

"But I thought you took the trip before he was bor—Oh. I see."

"I wasn't paying attention to the date when we had to stop in Meridian, but after that encounter with the officers in Jackson, sickness crashed over me like a runaway freight train. As we pulled off here in Edwards so I could get some air, your G'pop mentioned the date aloud because it was *his* late father's birthday. That's when I realized I was three days overdue for my cycle. Knew right then that I was pregnant."

"Wow." Scoob is riveted now. "What happened?"

"Well, we were nervous about having a baby—certainly hadn't planned on one—but it was also exciting. Problem was, we didn't know if we'd be able to find a doctor who would treat a white woman carrying a black man's child where we were headed. So we turned our RV around."

"Dang." Were there really *doctors* who would turn away a woman with a baby in her stomach? "That's deep, G'ma."

"It was a haaaaard decision, kiddo. We knew returning to Atlanta might be trouble for a number of reasons—some your G'pop wasn't even aware of. But we also knew we'd have a doctor. Jimmy said he'd never forgive himself if something happened to the baby. So that was that."

"Trip over," Scoob says, really feeling it.

"Indeed."

The sound of other vehicles whizzing by fills the cab, and G'ma peers over at Scoob. Which makes him wonder if she's about to call him the wrong name, or crumple again.

But then she smiles. "This is the furthest I've ever gotten, Scoob-a-doob."

He can't help but smile back. For the first time since they started the journey, she looks really and truly *happy*. "Congrats, G'ma."

She blushes and spins her chair around. "I'm gonna take a quick potty break and freshen up, if you don't mind. Then we'll be on our way."

"Cool."

Once she disappears into the bathroom, Scoob tries to sift through some of the new stuff he's learned and get his bearings. Yeah, G'ma's happy—which does make *Scoob* happy . . .

But the word *contraband* still hasn't left his mind from when they were in front of the Evers house.

And now there's more: mentions of *trouble* and *reasons* for not returning to Atlanta. Which reminds him of *pickpocketing, petty theft,* and *poor decisions.*

There's stuff G'pop *wasn't even aware of,* and strange sleep talk about *fixing it . . .*

Shifting license plates and suspicious diamond earrings.

By the time she slips back into the driver's seat, grinning at him like it's going out of style, all Scoob's questions have condensed into one: *Who even is my G'ma?*

To Scoob's surprise, G'ma decides to pass Vicksburg. "Nothin' here but a Civil War memorial, and I think you and I have had enough *P*-US history for the day."

She holds her nose when she says this.

But the sun's begun to sink by the time they cross the state line and stop for tacos in Monroe, Louisiana. So he's not surprised at all when she says she needs "a nap" and they head to an RV park right after. (Who knew there were so many!)

As soon as she vanishes behind her bed curtain, leaving Scoob at the table drawing in the margins of his map, he's made a decision: he's going to call Dad.

He waits until he can hear her faint snores before creeping to the cab of the RV and easing into the driver's seat. He slowly reaches into the door . . .

The phone isn't there.

He looks all around him. Checks every possible spot: cup holders, center console, glove box.

Nothing.

Did she *hide* it? Yeah, she was being weird about him making a call earlier, and, okay fine, has been weird about the phone in general, especially when it comes to Dad. But would she really put it somewhere he couldn't find it? What if there was an emergency and he needed to call 911? Surely she considered that.

Didn't she?

Bewildered, Scoob returns to the live-in part and, quietly, *carefully* checks every place of concealment he can see: cabinets, drawers, anything that opens. There's no phone, but Scoob does make an unexpected discovery in the hidden space behind the kitchen TV: rubber-banded piles—four of them—of crudely stacked green paper rectangles.

Money.

He pulls his hand back like something's bitten him and shoves the TV back into place.

Then he plops down into the dining booth. G'ma groans, but it barely even registers.

In a way, Scoob guesses it makes sense for her to have a lot of cash—she *did* just sell her house, and that's all he's ever seen her use to pay for stuff.

But then that word pops into his head again, with gusto this time: *contraband*.

This definitely feels contraband-y.

Or is he overthinking? He does know it suddenly makes sense why parents don't want their kids watching R-rated movies—his imagination's running *wild*. Which is not helpful in this moment. What if she, like . . . robbed a bank right before she came and got him?

He's gotta do *something*. Heading to a neighboring camper or the campground offices to ask for a phone to use seems a little extreme—this isn't exactly life-or-death. At least he doesn't *think* it is . . .

Besides, after flipping through the Green Book, which is safely back beneath his pillow, and hearing

G'ma's stories about the olden days, Scoob's not sure he wants to walk around this campground alone. Yes, there were five whole safe places listed in Monroe, Louisiana, but still: everyone he's seen at this campground so far has looked like G'ma. And there's no forgetting the way those people were glaring at him in that Alabama restaurant just two days ago.

He sighs and lets his head drop back. Which is when his eyes fall on G'ma's treasure chest beside the kitchen sink. Normally he wouldn't snoop around in her stuff, but . . . maybe she slipped the phone in there while he wasn't looking.

He takes a super-deep breath, glances at the bedspace curtain one more time, and rises to grab the box. Decides to take it up into his bunk to scope it out because at least then he's got his *own* curtain to hide behind and will have time to stash it if she happens to get up while he's committing what feels like breaking and entering.

Once he's sequestered away, he closes his eyes and sends a silent apology in G'ma's direction, then holds his breath as he lifts the lid. Slowly, carefully, *quietly,* Scoob removes G'ma's most treasured relics piece by piece and lays them out on his bunk.

Things he didn't notice before: a weirdly large silver coin—half dollar it says (when the heck was *that* a thing?); a piece of heavy paper the size and shape of a credit card that, upon reading, Scoob discovers is G'ma's old driver's license; a stack of business cards rubber-banded together, all of which appear to be from jewelry stores; and there's the thin gold necklace he saw her lay on the table earlier. The charm looks like a miniature skeleton key like the one Shenice has for the trunk that belonged to her great-grandfather, who was apparently some big-deal baseball player.

Then he's looking down into maroon velvet.

The pink diamond earrings aren't there. Which is comforting but also terrifying: What if his mind is playing tricks on him?

Also the opposite of comforting: there's no phone.

A burst of fury shoots up from Scoob's belly like a geyser to the brain. He hates everything and wants this dumb trip to be over.

After shoving all G'ma's junk toward the bunk's back wall—there's no way he's putting any of it back right now—and lying on his back, Scoob shuts his eyes. One thing's for sure: William "Scoob" Lamar's never felt so far from home.

Back to Sleep

Speaking of home, the next time Scoob *opens* his eyes, he seems to be back there. When he arrived, he's not sure—can't say he remembers the return journey—but there are all his most familiar things: impeccably neat entryway, empty peach bowl on the table . . .

Dad.

Scoob smiles: Dad's reclined in his La-Z-Boy with his hands tucked behind his head and his eyes closed, listening to his favorite Smokey Robinson and the Miracles album—"This is *real* music, son. What you know about that?"—in front of a crackling fire. Humming along like he doesn't have a care in the world.

Much less a son he hasn't spoken to in days.

Nervous, Scoob creeps down the low-lit hallway. Despite Dad's clearly chill demeanor in this moment, Scoob's seen the switch flip before: cool, calm, and collected to furious in a matter of moments. Dad's never laid a hand on Scoob before—doesn't believe in *corporal punishment,* as he calls it ("I taught him that," G'ma once told Scoob)—but the *ice* that rolls off Dad when he's angry . . . well, Scoob hates how small it makes him feel.

He stands right in front of the chair. "Umm. Hey, Dad."

No response. Dad doesn't even flinch.

Scoob raises his voice a bit. "Dad. I'm . . . I'm back, Dad."

Nothing.

Maybe he's asleep? Scoob steps right up to the chair, his heartbeat thundering in his ears like an angry storm. "Hey, Dad?"

Dad hums for a few seconds, moving his head in time to the music, and when he stops, he smiles.

Scoob takes a deep breath. Then gulps. Reaches his hand out to touch Dad's shoulder.

Except his hand never connects with anything solid. Holding it up to his face, Scoob realizes with a start: he can see right through it.

Scoob looks down at his arms and torso and legs and feet then. It's all see-through. *He's* all see-through. Rushing into the hall bathroom, Scoob flips the light on and looks in the mirror.

He doesn't have a reflection.

Like a ghost.

Out the door and around a corner into his room—which doesn't look like his room at all. There's a reddish-brown desk—same *mahogany* as G'ma's treasure box—where his bed should be. Book-filled shelves line the walls where he'd normally see his superhero posters. Instead of *his* personal treasure chest, which is full of his action figures, Lego sets, and collection of obsolete computer parts Dad has given him, there's a fancy-looking high-backed chair and ottoman.

Scoob rushes to the kitchen to check *his* personal pantry shelf. The one with his cereals and fruit snacks and the S'mores Pop-Tarts Dad wishes Scoob wouldn't eat but buys anyway.

There's nothing but a box of Grape-Nuts, a container of dry quinoa, and a gallon Ziploc bag of muesli (barf).

Even the board where Dad scribbles Scoob's daily instructions is gone.

Every trace of Scoob seems to have been erased. It's like he never even lived here.

"DAD!" he shouts then, tripping over his not-even-solid feet as he makes his way back to the living room. "Dad, please hear me!"

"I'm *so* sorry, Jimmy!" Dad says. His body isn't moving, but his mouth is.

Though it's not his voice.

It's G'ma's.

"What? Dad, it's me, Scoob! It's *William,* Dad. Your *son*—"

"I did the wrong thing, but I'm gonna make it up to you, Jimmy," Dad says in G'ma's voice again, turning to look at Scoob this time. Well . . . *through* him, apparently.

Scoob stumbles back. Dad's eyes are pure white, no irises or pupils or anything.

"We're already past where you and I got to before, William and me," Dad continues. "You would just love William to pieces, Jimmy. He's the best grandson there is. Reminds me of the best parts of you." Dad rises from the chair with a pillow in hand and walks toward Scoob.

"D-Dad . . . Wha . . . what are you doing?" Scoob stumbles backward and falls as Dad advances on him, pillow held at the edges with both hands. He leans over and lowers it toward his son's face.

Scoob squeezes his eyes shut.

"I just—I hope you'll forgive me one day, Jimmy," Dad is saying. "I'll never forgive myself, but I hope you'll forgive me. I'm gonna make it this time, and I'll do what we planned, and then you'll forgive me—"

"DAD!" The sound is muffled.

Scoob can't breathe. He twists and kicks and flails—

And when he finally manages to inhale, his eyelids snap open and there are tears running down into his ears. He bolts upright, desperately thirsty and wanting to go to Dad, but smacks his head on the low ceiling of his bunk. "OW!" he shouts.

"Jimmy?" comes G'ma's voice from the other end of the RV. "Jimmy, are you all right? Jimmy . . ." The sound trails off, and soon Scoob is hearing her soft snores again.

He breathes in deep and tries to get his heart to slow down. Holds his hands up to his face, and he can tell they're solid now even though it's dark. He's gotta pull it together.

It was just a dream, Scoob. You're fine—

Wait.

It's dark.

Scoob flips to his belly to look out of his small window. Again: a bajillion and one stars. It was just creeping into dusk when he fell asleep, which means—what time is it? He moves to climb down and check, but something crunches beneath him.

One of G'ma's road maps.

It all comes tumbling back into his head then: contraband and G'ma acting weird and piles of money behind the TV.

G'ma's missing phone.

Scoob swallows hard—he really wishes he had some water—and blinks back a wave of . . . well, he's not sure what exactly. A few things hit him at once: he's trapped at some campground in Monroe, Louisiana (according to the map—without which he would have *no idea* where the heck he is), with no phone and no idea when he's going home.

And he really, *really* misses Dad. Like more than he's ever missed anybody.

Especially after that horrible dream.

Though what he can do about it, Scoob doesn't have a clue.

He sighs and lies back down. Imagines the tire swing behind G'ma's old house and playing with Shenice on it.

Then he drifts back to sleep.

To Mexico

This time Scoob is pulled from slumber by the fatty fragrance of bacon.

Which would normally be great, but right now he's literally *lying on* pieces of G'ma's greatest treasures. That photo of G'pop beneath the old hotel marquee in Meridian? It's dented in the middle and has drool crusted over half of the guy's face.

Not good.

He *gently* shifts—doesn't want G'ma to know he's up until he can at least get all her stuff back in the treasure chest. He'll sneak it back down and slip it in a drawer while she's in the bathroom or something. Hopefully she hasn't noticed it's missing.

The lid creaks as Scoob's lowering it to secure the latch, and he freezes. Thankfully there's no reaction from below. He shoves the chest as far into a bunk corner as he can, then takes a preparation breath before shifting his curtain aside to climb down.

The driver's-side door of the RV opens the moment Scoob's feet touch the floor.

He literally jumps *and* yelps like a scared toddler.

G'ma sticks her head into the cab. "You all right there, kiddo?"

For a second, they just stare at each other because Scoob can't get his mouth to move. Too many responses—some true, some not—are colliding in his head and breaking up into floating letters he can't seem to wrangle back into words that make sense.

Then she shrugs and climbs into the driver's seat. "Left your breakfast in the microwave. Go on and grab it and sit down at the table so I can get us moving here." As soon as the door is shut, the rabid funk of cigarette smoke assaults Scoob's nose.

That smacks him out of it.

"G'ma, I'd really like to call my dad, if you don't mind," Scoob says, striding right up to the passenger seat to sit beside her as she cranks the RV.

"I don't mind," she says. Words so surprising to Scoob, they blow him back in his seat. He hopes she doesn't notice.

"You don't?"

"Not in the least."

"Okay . . ."

"Don't have a phone, though." The camper thunks into gear, and G'ma shoots out of their campsite space with more force than Scoob expects.

"You . . . what now?"

"I got rid of it," she says with a wave of her hand like it's the most trivial thing on planet Earth. "Wasn't working right, so I threw it in the garbage."

"You threw your *phone* in the garbage?"

She nods once. Resolutely. "Sure did. Didn't need a phone the first time I took this trip, and don't need one now. Got maps in my keepsake box, and I just snagged a current one from the campground front office."

Scoob is *astonished,* as Shenice likes to say.

(He really misses that girl.)

158

"Speaking of which, have you *seen* my keepsake box anywhere?" she says. "Coulda sworn it was on the counter before I lay down yesterday, but when I went to look for my old Louisiana map, I couldn't find the thing. Checked all the drawers and cabinets, too."

"Oh, uhh . . ." Well, no point in lying. At least not completely: "I put it in my bunk. For safekeeping."

He braces himself for fury or suspicion or disappointment—*something* unpleasant—from her.

But when she turns to him, she's beaming. "Well, what a good wingman you are, Scoob-a-doob! I mean that in the military sense, by the way. Not the way young folks these days use it." She snorts. "Relying on a friend to test the waters when you're looking for a date? Amateurs."

Despite his mood, this makes Scoob chuckle.

"Anyway, so glad you're keeping our treasure protected," she continues. "So responsible!"

Responsible. Dad's favorite word ever in the history of language.

Which brings Scoob back to the matter at hand. "G'ma, you sure it was a good idea to throw your phone out? What if there's an emergency?"

"Oh, we'll be fiiiiine. Since when are you such a worrywart?"

"I just mean . . ." Scoob gulps as pieces of his dream—and what it could mean—stalk through his head boogeyman-style. "How's Dad supposed to get in touch with us? Or us with him?"

"*We* with him, William."

Is she really correcting his grammar? Scoob has to swallow and clear his throat to do away with the *WHO EVEN ARE YOU, LADY?* that tries to leap from his mouth.

He presses on. "I'm not worried, G'ma." Pure lies. "But *Dad* will be. And like . . . if I'm missing school, I'll at least need to call Shenice to get the homework."

"Lordy, you sound just *like* your stick-in-the-mud father! We're on a whirlwind adventure here, Scoob-a-doob! Homework, schmomework!"

An *adventure*, huh?

"I'm just saying, G'ma," Scoob goes on, deciding to run with this particular train of thought. It's as good a way as any to try and get some solid answers out of her. "Exactly how many days of school do you think I'll miss? We should be back home what, Thursday or so?"

She grins in that I-know-something-you-don't kinda way grown-ups do sometimes.

It's a grin Scoob's not fond of right now. Not when she's trying to justify trashing their sole means of communication while reeking of cigarette smoke. He can't even look at her anymore. It's like the woman he's spent his whole life looking up to has been replaced with a total stranger.

"All shall be well, kiddo," she says—a grown-up nonanswer.

"But, G'ma—"

"Besides"—she cuts him off—"home is where you make it."

An hour and a half farther across Louisiana—which isn't as far as one would think considering their minimum-speed-limit pace—G'ma turns the music down and signals to exit the freeway. Gas gauge is practically on *E*.

"Scoob-a-doob, didya know the Louisiana state song is 'You Are My Sunshine'?" she asks.

Scoob did know that. It's one of the five Louisiana Fun Facts staring up at him from a small box in the top right corner of the Louisiana section of his map—fun facts he's been reading and illustrating all over the state for who knows how long. A couple others: (1) the highest point in the state is Mount Driskill at 535 feet above sea level—which is less than 2 percent of the height of Mount Everest; and (2) the state flower is the magnolia. "Yeah. It's pretty cool."

"Wanna hear something else about Louisiana?" They turn right.

"Sure." Cuz why not?

"This is the state where a girl—named Ruby like me—was the first black person to go to a white school here in the South."

"Wait . . ." *No way.* "You mean Ruby *Bridges*?"

"Oh, you know of her, then!"

"Dad told me about her in fourth grade." Scoob looks all around him. There are banks and restaurants. Gas stations. Even a Walmart Supercenter. And he knows it was a long time ago, but to think a thing like *that* happened in a place as normal-looking as *this* . . . "That happened *here*?" he says.

"Not *here,* here in Shreveport, no. New Orleans. But it was still a big deal for the state. Prior to her first day in 1960, schools in this part of the country were completely segregated."

G'ma turns into a gas station and parks at a pump. And as she reaches for the door handle, the truth smacks Scoob: "G'ma!"

Her eyebrows lift. "Yes, William?"

He has to turn and look at her. "Your school had only white kids when you were my age?"

"Yep."

Whoa. "What was that even *like*?"

She shrugs. "It was my normal. Didn't think any-thing of it when I was in it."

"So you didn't have *any* black friends when you were a kid?"

"Not a one."

"Dang."

"But enough about that now." She pats his knee. "Let's not dwell on the past, hmm? Hop on down so we can grab refreshments while the gas is pumping."

Scoob does as he's told.

But he winds up regretting it. Because as *soon* as they step inside the convenience store, the white clerk behind the counter looks between him and G'ma, and her eyes narrow.

He *refuses* to look away this time. Even when, without taking her eyes off him, said clerk tugs the sleeve of a different clerk, whispers something to him, and then *he* looks in Scoob and G'ma's direction. Suspiciously.

"Strawberry or Brown Sugar Cinnamon Pop-Tarts, kiddo?" G'ma calls out, none the wiser.

He sighs and heads to where she's studying options in the unhealthy-snack aisle.

"You pick, G'ma."

She turns to study his face. "You all right, Scoob-a-doob?"

"Yeah." Can't face her as he lies, so he pretends to skim the potato chip options. "I'm fine—"

Except he's *really* not fine now because he can see the male clerk "restocking" something nearby. And the guy keeps peeping in Scoob and G'ma's direction.

Scoob's had enough. "I'm gonna get some air." And he walks away—eye-stabbing *both* clerks—before G'ma can say a word.

She unlocks the RV as she exits the store, and

Scoob climbs in and sits fuming while she replaces the gas pump. Probably should've offered to do it for her but . . . well, he's not in the mood.

The second she's in her seat, she looks in his direction and opens her mouth to speak, but he beats her to it: "G'ma, how'd you and G'pop meet?"

She blinks. Like she's caught off guard. "Filling station," she says. "Why do you ask?"

"Where's that? Were you catching a train or something?"

Now she laughs. "We're *at* a filling station. Guess you call them gas stations now."

"Oh." Ironic.

"He was workin' at one," she says. "Pumping gas. Wanted nothing at all to do with me at first." She shakes her head, but she's into her story now. "I tell ya, Scoob-a-doob: the excuses I came up with to visit that station as often as possible. Whew! Wore him down little by little, though."

"What made you want to . . . *date* him? Especially back then." Scoob decides to just go ahead and say what's on his mind: "I'm sure you knew people would be opposed to it, right? Why put yourself through pain for someone you didn't know?" He's really hoping she doesn't say *love at first sight* or something bananas like that.

"Dunno" is her response. With a shrug. "There was something about him that wouldn't let me go. Stayed true for as long as we were together. Wasn't bad to look at, either." She winks.

Gross.

Scoob shakes it off. "So what'd he go to jail for? Like, I know it was—"

"Grand larceny."

"Uhh—"

"Theft."

"Yeah, but what'd he steal?"

She doesn't respond at first, but he's got a hunch that she will. She's got her baby blues all squinched up behind her glasses, and she *worrying*—as he's heard her say when *he's* doing it—her bottom lip between her teeth.

Then she shifts her focus out the window. "His conviction involved money and jewelry, but—" She sighs. "It's complicated, Scoob-a-doob. Bottom line, he was unjustly imprisoned. Yes, he did some stealing, and yes, stealing is wrong. But *he* didn't steal everything the police said he did."

She doesn't go on. Scoob's turn to be response-
less now.

"We just need to get to Juárez," she says, suddenly energized. She puts the RV in gear.

Scoob opens his mouth to speak but changes his
mind.

There's nothing left to say.

"Everything will be fine then."

They're going.

"We'll get there and I'll finish—" She sits up
straighter. "We just gotta get to Mexico."

THE LONE STAR STATE

STATE MOTTO
"Friendship."

TEXAS

STATE TREE
Pecan

AUSTIN

STATE FLOWER
Bluebonnet

STATE BIRD
Mockingbird

FUN FACT
TEXAS CHILI DOESN'T HAVE BEANS.

Best Day Ever

They cross into Texas and drive for a while without stopping. Which is a huge relief to Scoob, knowing they're finally making some real progress on this . . . *journey,* he guesses it is.

Scoob's seen the map: the city they're headed to is literally right across the border. His new hope is that once they make it to Juárez and G'ma *fixes* or *finishes* or *makes* whatever *it* is *right,* her conscience will be so clear, her hair will turn green like go or something, and she'll be so relieved, they'll hop back into the RV and hightail it home. After another gas run and pause for lunch seventeen miles outside of

Dallas—at least according to the sign they've just passed—they push on.

It's . . . nice. Scoob's got his window down, and the fresh air gusting into his face as they gobble miles and miles of Texas open road clears his head in a way he doesn't expect.

He actually falls asleep. Which he only discovers when G'ma touches his leg and he jerks awake so hard, both arms fly into the air and he squawks like a startled chicken.

G'ma laughs. Hard. "Sleeping good?"

"Not funny, G'ma," Scoob says rubbing his eyes.

"Well, if you'll indulge me one final stop on this trek of ours, I'll make the interrupted slumber worth your while."

Another stop.

"I'd like to fulfill what's been a dream of mine for a very long time."

"Oh." Scoob sits up in his seat, fully alert now. "Okay."

She doesn't say anything else until they're taking an exit into Arlington. It's the exit for—

No way.

"G'ma, are we going to *Six Flags*?"

When she looks at him this time, Scoob sees her: *his* G'ma. The one he's known his whole life.

The biggest belly laugh ever bubbles out of him.

"I knew you'd be into it," she says. "It's why you're my favorite grandson." She makes her white eyebrows dance.

There's no expressing how good it feels to have her back.

Scoob has to say: he's never seen G'ma this *awestruck* before. She looks like one of those white kids in Christmas movies who wake up to a tree packed with presents underneath—like the whole world was just handed to her on a gold-rimmed plate.

"We gotta find the Runaway Mine Train, Scooba-doob," she says. "The Six Flags we have in Georgia opened in sixty-seven, and one of *their* premier rides was the Dahlonega Mine Train. Runaway's the Texas version."

"Wait, really?" Scoob's never been to Six Flags over Georgia, but he's heard of the Dahlonega Mine Train.

"Yep! As your G'pop and I passed *that* park on

our way out of Atlanta, I was sad. Knew I'd never get to experience a place like that with him. There wasn't a theme park in the South that would've permitted it."

Now Scoob is sad too.

"But there's redemption!" she practically shouts. "When you and me stopped for gas not too long ago, I noticed an old poster for *this* Six Flags on one of the walls. Had a mine train ride on it and everything."

Now Scoob is smiling. G'ma *would* notice a random poster in a gas station.

"Asked the attendant about it, and he told me the thing's still in operation. *'Oldest coaster in the park!'* he said. I knew right then we'd have to stop."

Scoob consults the map and they get to walking, but as soon as they're standing in front of the entrance and he sees how rickety the ride looks, he feels like his stomach has dropped down to his ankle region.

"Umm . . . ," Scoob murmurs as a question pops into his head—in Dad's voice. "How exactly old is this 'coaster'?"

"Built in sixty-six, according to the fella! Ain't

that amazing? It was here when your G'pop and I started on our trip! Would've passed right by it had we made it this far!"

1966? It's older than Dad!

That's . . . really old. For a roller coaster.

"You sure this thing is safe, G'ma?" Scoob says as they step into the line. A line that isn't very long. Which doesn't seem like a good sign.

"Oh, don't be such a killjoy!" she says. "You think they'd let people on the thing if it wasn't safe? Nobody wants a lawsuit, Scoob-a-doob."

He guesses she's got a point there.

"Come on!"

After a fifteen-minute wait—during which G'ma bounces on the balls of her tiny feet like she's never been so excited in her life—they climb into the very front coaster car. (Oh boy.)

Despite the fact that the thing squawks and groans like it's complaining about having a bad back the moment Scoob and G'ma sit down, and the initial takeoff is so jerky that Scoob feels like his lunch is about to reappear in his trousers, once they're fully

in motion, the ride winds up being pretty fun. He's sure it's partially due to G'ma's *whoop*s and *whee*s and squeals of glee from beside him, but by the time they get off, he's feeling pretty exhilarated.

"Let's find a BIGGER one!" G'ma shouts, her pouf of white hair standing up all over her head like she stuck a butter knife in a toaster. (Scoob did that once. He doesn't recommend it.)

"A bigger what?"

"COASTER!" And she throws her hands in the air.

So they do.

There's the Shock Wave—Scoob has no idea what Gs are, but the ride promises five-point-nine of them, and based on how his heart flip-flops around inside his body, he'd say it delivers.

And then the Joker—a strange one for sure. They spend more time upside down than right side up.

The Titan's massive drop makes Scoob feel like his brain got left back at the top of the metal hill.

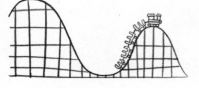

And on. And on.

When he and G'ma step up to the Superman: Tower of Power—what they've decided will be their final ride—Scoob's eyebrows shoot up to his hairline. He has to tilt his head back as far as it'll go to see the top of the thing.

And the whole experience winds up being *way* worse than he expects: he's pretty sure his lungs stay on the ground as they *shoot* thirty-two stories into the air, and he definitely dies for a few seconds during the drop.

But once their feet are back on the ground?

He hugs G'ma so tight she yelps. "Don't break me, kiddo!"

He lets go and looks her right in the eye. "G'ma?"

"Yes?"

"Thank you."

"What for?"

He hugs her again. "For making this the best day ever."

Caught Red-Handed

Within fifteen minutes of getting back on the road, exhaustion drops onto Scoob with so much weight, the thought of even lifting his arms seems *outlandish*. (Another Dad word. Guy's taking over Scoob's brain).

He vaguely remembers G'ma saying, "Kiddo, I think we might have to park it for the night," though how and when he winds up in his bunk—freshly showered, it seems—for the night, he's not sure.

When Scoob wakes, though, the RV is in motion. He peeks out his window, and the fog instantly clears from his brain: it's pitch dark outside.

"G'ma?" he says, not alert enough to get a lid on his panic.

"Go back to sleep, kiddo."

"What time is it? Why are we driving at night?"

"Sleep, child. Don't you worry about all of that."

"But aren't *you* tired, G'ma?"

"I'm fine, I'm fine. Grabbed a few of those 5-Hour ENERGY things when I checked us out of the campground. Go on to sleep now. That's an order."

So he does.

The next time his eyes open, something feels . . . off.

It's too quiet.

He startles, and his foot—missing a sock—strikes something hard and sharp-edged. He groans and instinctively rolls to his side.

Almost falls right off the edge of the bunk.

"Whoa!" he says, quickly shifting back and putting a hand over his chest to try and slow his breathing *and* heart rate down.

Then he sees what he kicked: G'ma's treasure chest. Which in this moment is giving him a serious case of the creeps.

He shifts his bunk curtain and sees that the one around G'ma's bed is closed. But he doesn't hear her snoring.

"G'ma? You asleep?"

No reply.

"Uhhh, G'ma?"

Still nothing. Which he hopes doesn't mean . . .

He gulps and climbs down.

When he pulls the very edge of her curtain back, he almost passes out.

From relief.

The bed is perfectly made. And perfectly empty.

But where the heck is she? And (almost) more importantly: Where are *they*? Still in Texas?

He looks out the dining booth window. Sun's high in the sky and there's a gas station a short distance away, but the lot where the RV is parked is otherwise abandoned.

"Where'd you go, G'ma?"

In the barely visible reflection from the window glass, Scoob notices a white rectangle on the fridge beneath the Six Flags over Texas magnet G'ma bought, and whips around. It's got his name on it in that loopy scrawl of G'ma's, though there are places where the edges of letters go jagged or flat, and even a place where she was pressing down so hard, she poked a hole in the paper.

Strange.

He pulls it off:

My beloved William,

    Welcome to Abilene, TX!

    I ran out for some fresh air and to find us a new map. Failed to grab one during our last gas stop, and according to my old map, this is the last decent-sized city we'll pass through for a while.

    I left the generator on, and there's cereal in the cabinet and food in the fridge if you're hungry. TV remote is in the top drawer below the cooktop.

             Love,

             G'ma Ruby Jean

Scoob returns the note to the table and stares at the vast concrete wasteland surrounding the RV and sighs.

180

After three bowls of Corn Pops, two smoked turkey and manchego sandwiches (gotta love the fancy grandma cheese), and a bathroom break that required half a can of air freshener and three open windows, G'ma still hasn't returned.

So he takes her other sort-of-suggestion and turns on the TV.

The antenna only picks up four channels. One is religious, if the cowboy-looking guy hopping around a purple carpeted stage and adding *ah* to every third word of what he's saying is any indication: *And I said-ah, the good Lord-ah, he is among us-ah.*

Then there's a channel entirely in Spanish playing what is surely a sappy soap opera.

The final two appear to be local channels There's a television judge on one, going off on some bad roommate who ran up a water bill too high, and the other is playing a show where four ladies are sitting around a table, talking.

He leaves it tuned there and goes to his backpack for the road map. Circle some spots on the route and draw in some doodles— cowboy hat, roller coaster, giant tower of death—just for something to do.

He's putting the finishing touches on the fifth of six flags when a loud and piercing *BEEEEEEEEEEEEEEEP* sounds from the TV. The words **AMBER ALERT** begin scrolling across the bottom of the screen as the picture cuts to a newsroom. Curious, Scoob increases the volume as the somber-looking newscaster dude starts talking.

"In breaking news, we interrupt your regularly scheduled programming with an emergency message. The City of Atlanta Police Department has issued a Multi-State Amber Alert for an eleven-year-old boy last seen entering a recreational vehicle outside his home this past Friday. The boy is believed to be with Ruby Jean Lamar, his seventy-six-year-old grandmother, who is currently under investigation in connection with a string of thefts involving jewelry stores in the Atlanta area.

"The boy's father said he last spoke to Ms. Lamar on Saturday, and that while he had no direct contact with the boy, he has reason to believe his son is in Ms. Lamar's care. A cell phone formerly in Ms. Lamar's possession was located at a campground in Monroe, Louisiana, shortly before authorities received an anonymous tip from two gas station employees in Shreveport. Based on recent surveillance video from a Subway store just outside Dallas, Texas, Ms. Lamar is believed to be headed west across the Lone Star State with her grandson in tow."

If not for the pictures that appear on the screen, Scoob would've assumed there was a second Ruby Jean Lamar out in the world somewhere. But there's no denying the school photo Scoob took this past October, and an image of G'ma from a Fourth of July barbecue last year—which he knows because he took the picture.

"If you have any information regarding the whereabouts of William Lamar and/or Ruby Jean Lamar, please call the number on the screen below."

The *BEEEEEEEEEEEEEEEEEP* sounds again, and then the TV cuts back to the chatting ladies. Scoob stares at the center of the screen without actually seeing anything.

He has to get some air.

Now.

He's vaguely conscious of his weight shifting to his feet, and then the coolness against his palm from the metal of the door latch.

Then there's hot air smudged with cigarette smoke hitting his face.

The moment Scoob's foot touches down on the concrete, he hears a gasp.

And there's G'ma. Putting out a lit cigarette against the side of her new sweet ride. She's got a whole pack in her other hand.

They make eye contact and she freezes.

Scoob stops breathing.

"Oh boy," G'ma says.

Scoob couldn't respond if he tried.

"Guess I'm caught red-handed."

Get Settled

Smoking, is what she means.

Scoob caught her *smoking* red-handed.

"You can't tell your dad, Scoob-a-doob," she says as she turns the key to crank the Winnebago. "I'll never hear the end of it."

"Okay."

In truth, Scoob couldn't be more relieved about finding G'ma putting out what she confessed was her seventh cigarette. Gives a nice excuse for his silence.

And he is dead silent. All he can think about is *Multi-State Amber Alert* and *under investigation* and *string of thefts*. Though he can't seem to get the words swallowed and down into his belly where they'll be properly digested and he can figure out what to *do*.

The theft part is one thing. After everything he's learned—and seen—he knows that part is definitely possible. *String* makes it sound like she went on some kinda spree, which seems like a stretch (she's seventy-six years old, for goodness' sake), but there's no denying she almost walked out of that store in Meridian with a ring.

He glances at her white hands on the steering wheel without turning his head. What if there really was a string? What'd she do with what she stole? Could it be here in the RV? Are they hauling *contraband* to Mexico?

Well . . . *contraband* in addition to *him*. Because that's the other thing: Scoob *knows* what *Amber Alert* means.

A kid's been kidnapped.

Now he looks at his own hands. His brown ones. Which he's learned from this trip means so much more than he knew. Scoob doesn't *feel* kidnapped. Wouldn't he be more scared for his life or something? Kidnappers are creepy dudes in old vans, not a kid's favorite (only) grandma. . . .

His head turns toward her without his permission. She certainly *looks* like the sweet little lady who cleaned his boo-boos and cooked his favorite food and helped with his homework and let him do stuff Dad wouldn't. The woman who's always been his personal heroine.

Kidnappers take kids without permission and hold them against their will. Scoob's here because he wants to be.

And he *knows* that if he asked her to take him home right this second, she would.

Wouldn't she?

She turns to him then.

Scoob expects her to speak but she doesn't.

He wants to say something but can't.

So they just . . . stare. And then she smiles. In a way that isn't much of a smile at all.

By the time they stop again—"for the night," G'ma says, and it gives Scoob a chill, but he doesn't argue—he still hasn't figured out what to say. Or *do*.

It's been almost four hours.

They park and get hooked up. The campsite is full of sand dunes and seems to be in the middle of a desert; no major city within a hundred miles, so Scoob doesn't need the Green Book to tell him this would *not* have been a safe place for someone like him during G'ma's first trip.

Not that it matters. If you let the Amber Alert people tell it, Scoob's in danger no matter *where* he is right now.

"Have a sit-down, Scoob-a-doob," G'ma says. "I'll make you a hot chocolate."

There's no way Scoob can stomach one of G'ma's super-rich hot chocolates now, but he sits down anyway because what else is he supposed to do?

As she rotates away from him, Scoob can't help but look around for all the places it might be possible to stash stolen jewelry. He didn't find anything suspicious back when searching high and low for G'ma's phone, but still. So many drawers and cabinets, nooks and crannies. He's pretty sure there's even a storage space beneath the booth bench he's sitting on.

When his gaze locks in on the TV, he remembers the money hidden behind it. Is that stolen too?

No clue how long he sits staring at the darkened screen, but soon G'ma's setting a steaming mug down in front  of him. She slides onto the bench opposite and clasps her wrinkly hands around a cup of water. She smiles, but her eyeballs are shiny . . .

Scoob drops his eyes to her glass and clears his throat. "No cocoa for you?"

"Nah," she says. "Just thought you could use a reminder of home."

"Oh."

"I know I've said it plenty, but I need to say it one final time," she continues while he burns a hole in the table with his laser stare. "I'm thankful you're here with me, Scoob-a-doob. It means the whole world to me. Wouldn't've gotten this far without you. I mean it."

Scoob forces his gaze up. She's staring out the window with her shoulders so stooped, he wonders if she'll ever sit straight and tall again.

And maybe it's the sorrow Scoob can imagine making the lines in her face look deeper. Or the twitch in her hands that makes her water quake in her cup. Or the fact that her head is hanging so heavily, Scoob's afraid her neck won't support it for much longer.

Maybe it's all of those things taken together.

"I'm gonna hit the hay," she says, slowly rising and placing her half-empty glass of water on the kitchenette counter. Then she ambles to her sleeping corner and vanishes behind the curtain.

That's when Scoob knows: there's something very wrong with his G'ma.

He wakes soaked in sweat.

"Jimmy?"

Scoob pushes up onto an elbow and slides his curtain open. G'ma's is closed, though he can hear her shifting around behind it.

He lets his head fall back onto his pillow.

G'ma calls out again: "I've got a bad feeling, Jimmy."

"Yeah, me too," Scoob says under his breath.

Before going to bed himself, Scoob went outside and took inventory of their surroundings. They're parked in Monahans Sandhills State Park, and while the two sites adjacent to theirs were empty when he checked, there was a tour bus–sized RV parked on the other side of the nearest dune.

He flips to look out the window and make sure it's still there.

"Jimmy? Jimmy, where are ya? We have to go now."

Her voice is louder this time. Scoob's tempted to put the pillow over his head but—

"Jimmy?"

—her voice is getting closer.

"No. No, no! It's all my fault! He didn't do—" There's a thump, followed by the sound of breaking glass, then, "Oh!"

Scoob throws the bunk curtain aside and clambers down. "G'ma!"

She's swaying with a hand on her forehead.

He knows *he's* in trouble when he takes a final step and a feeling like lightning shoots up his leg, but he catches her just as she collapses.

G'pop hadn't stolen any of the jewelry the police found when they raided his and G'ma's house in 1968.

G'ma had.

That's what she tells Scoob between sobs once she's able to talk. "I was so *stupid*," she says. "We'd been home over a month with no trouble, so I thought we were in the clear."

She's sitting on her bed, her back supported by the wall, with Scoob perched beside her, his hand clutched between her thin, trembly ones. He flinches as she squeezes his a little harder than he knew possible.

"I started stealing jewelry when I was twelve, and for the most part, I got away with it. Your grandfather had been secreting away money he was stealing from that filling station he worked at, as well as a couple other odd jobs of his, but he didn't know I'd been doing some work of my own. When I suggested we run away to Mexico, he thought it was solely because of what *he'd* been taking." She shakes her head.

"I should've gotten rid of it all before we even turned around, but . . . well, I don't know what I was thinking. Certainly didn't *want* to part with my spoils. I was an *angry* young woman, Scoob—my daddy left, and my mama passed away, and people were so *awful* to one another, especially white folks to blacks—and the stealing . . ." She pauses to take a breath. "Well, it was my way of gettin' back at the world. Just the *thought* of all the things I'd taken— silly trinkets I knew folks valued more than they did other human beings—it made me feel powerful. Felt good to do bad. And no one suspected the pretty blond girl with the 'megawatt smile' of being a professional jewel thief."

Professional jewel thief. That's an oxymoron if Scoob's ever heard one.

"The police came in the dead of the night," she continues. "They only found about four thousand dollars cash, which I think Jimmy might've been able to explain away if not for the jewelry. One of the pieces was a diamond tennis bracelet that I *knew* was too expensive to be written off by the store I took it from, but since we were leaving, I went for it anyway."

Her sobs intensify.

"Jimmy tried to tell 'em he hadn't taken the stuff,

but of course they didn't believe him. And they were doubly furious to find us *together*. Really. But I—I didn't say anything, Scoob . . ."

Oh.

"I *never* said anything. Yeah, he was gonna go to jail no matter what—back then, if you were black and accused of a crime, you were guilty whether you'd done it or not, and he really *had* stolen the money . . ."

Oh.

"But all these years, I've never shaken *my* guilt over Jimmy being convicted of something he *didn't* do."

Oh.

"*I* stole that jewelry, Scoob. Not him."

Oh.

"But I told myself coming clean would mean losing our baby. Kept myself convinced Jimmy wouldn't've wanted that. The more time passed without the police after *me,* the easier that was to believe. Also figured it'd cause *him* trouble with the white inmates if I showed up at the jailhouse.

"So I never went to visit."

Oh.

"Keeping the secret got harder as your dad got older and wanted to know more about his father," she continues, "and I kept my answers vague, but you know how your dad is. He dug up his own answers and drew his own conclusions about the type of man James Senior was."

"And you never corrected him," Scoob says.

She shakes her head. "Didn't have the courage. Your dad loved *me*, and I wanted it to stay that way, William. He was all I had. Jimmy got twenty-five *years* and there was no tellin' whether a confession from me would even have helped. System wasn't fair."

Isn't fair, Scoob thinks. Still.

"Jimmy *died* in that prison, Scoob. All because of me."

And there's nothing else to be said.

So after a silence that grows and morphs and shifts the entire landscape of Scoob's life, when G'ma says, "I need to lie down," Scoob helps her get settled.

Home

No one realizes the black boy with a piece of glass in his foot is the Amber Alert kid until Scoob and G'ma get to the hospital and they locate her ID. Which surprises him. No, he didn't give his real name or hers, but either they were in a remote-enough area that no one had heard the report, or old white ladies travel with little black boys all the time.

He really only lied because he didn't want cops to show up and handcuff her on the spot, but looking at her now with tubes sticking out of her arms and nose, he can see how silly that was—nobody with half a heart would arrest a sick old lady.

And sick she is. The doctors and nurses drop their voices super low and whisper to each other when Scoob's within earshot, so he doesn't have a clue what's actually *wrong* with her. But he does know that when Mr. Winston, the guy from the massive camper on the other side of the dune, followed Scoob back to check on G'ma, he immediately called 911.

It was Scoob's first time in an ambulance.

Also his first time getting stitches. They cleaned and rebandaged his elbow, too.

And now he's here. In a poorly lit room that smells like hand sanitizer on a sorry excuse for a recliner with his wrapped foot propped up. Everything around reminding him of how far he is from home.

From Dad.

Who will hopefully be here soon. Police showed up not too long ago, and Scoob told them he wanted to stay with G'ma. That she hadn't *kidnapped* him. That they were on a road trip and he was fine.

He's guessing they also had no idea what to do with him. So they left him be. For the time being, at least. All Scoob knows is the officer who asked the questions disappeared for a few minutes after getting Scoob's answers, then poked his head back in the room and said: *You can stay. We talked to your dad. He's on the way.*

Now all there's left for Scoob to do is watch over G'ma until Dad gets here.

He stares at her closed eyes and perfectly still upper body. Her paper-thin skin, so pale he wonders if they need to attach a bag of blood to one of those poles and give her a refill. He still hasn't really processed what she told him, but it's almost like spilling the truth just . . . emptied her completely.

Which is the reason he decided *he* didn't want to call Dad when the hospital people offered. He couldn't guarantee all the secrets G'ma dumped into him wouldn't surge back up and pour out.

When Scoob comes to he's been covered with a blanket, and the pillow his head is on is wet with drool. Sunlight streams through the window, filling the room like it's the rightful owner, and as soon as he gets his eyes all the way open, he has to shut them again. It's way too bright.

From the glimpse he caught, G'ma's in the same position she was the last time he saw her, the beeps and drips of her machines and IV steady.

He cracks his eyelids again. Looking at the bag with the clear liquid, it hits Scoob how thirsty he is. He needs to find some water. And food. And his neck is stiff from sleeping on what has to be Texas's most uncomfortable couch. (He is still in Texas, isn't he?) He doesn't even remember lying down.

His stomach growls angrily, and the hunger spreads up into his ribs. He shifts to his back and groans.

There's a response groan from the opposite side of the room.

Scoob freezes, eyes wide, heart thumping so fast, he knows if *he* were hooked up to the monitor, it would sound like a five-bell alarm.

Slowly, careful, Scoob lifts his head.

There in the chair—same one Scoob's pretty sure he fell asleep in last night—is a light-brown-skinned (or *beige,* as G'ma likes to say), bearded man with his hands clasped over his midsection, and legs so long, the recliner part hits him midcalf.

He's asleep, but he's still got his shoes and glasses on. (Typical.)

Dad.

Scoob's taken *way* aback by how quickly the air in his throat expands and his eyes fill with tears.

And of course as soon as the first ones spill onto his cheeks, Dad's eyes open. "William?" he says.

Then faster than Scoob can register the movement, his body is leaving the couch and he's wrapped in Dad's arms.

Dad—who's crying just as hard as Scoob is.

Home.

ROUTE
21

More Than They Have

Despite the twenty-one thousand trillion questions tussling in his head, Scoob doesn't say much as Dad drives him to a hotel near the hospital so he can "sleep in a *real* bed for a while."

He does ask the most important one, though it tries to choke him on its way out of his throat: "Is G'ma gonna be okay, Dad?"

Dad's neck muscles tighten. And his hands twist on the steering wheel of the rental car. The RV, Scoob learned, was *impounded,* which brings to mind stray animals trapped in cages and makes him a little bit angry—but perhaps that's because he knows he's not going to like what Dad's about to say.

The old man sighs, and his hands relax like all the fight's gone out of him. "She doesn't have long, William. I spoke with her doctor on Monday and, well . . ." He stops talking. Peeks at Scoob out of the corners of his eyes. "You sure you wanna hear this, son?"

Scoob nods.

So Dad nods too. "Your grandmother was diagnosed with pancreatic cancer six months ago—"

"Six *months* ago?"

"Mmhmm. And she told the doctor she didn't want treatment. Wanted to 'let it run its course.'" Dad shakes his head sadly. "Doc said she had no idea how your grandmother was even doing because Mom—G'ma—quit coming in for checkups. She'd already reached stage three, and—" Dad pauses to take a breath.

Scoob doesn't say a word.

"That means it was spreading fast, William," Dad says.

"But she seemed fine," comes Scoob's reply, unbidden. If people have *cancer,* shouldn't they seem sick?

"It's like that sometimes," Dad says with a shrug. "There aren't always symptoms you can see."

Now Scoob's eyes are wet again. He's pretty sure he's cried more over the past twenty-four hours than he has in his whole life. "So she's gonna die?"

The air in the car gets soupy, and Scoob can tell the question is hitting Dad harder than Scoob realized it would. Dad's always so . . . practical. One plus one is two.

Scoob turns to look at Dad, who in this moment is just . . . a sad man with a sick mom. And it occurs to him: this has gotta be harder for Dad than it is for Scoob. Yeah, G'ma's (still!) Scoob's favorite person in the galaxy . . . But Dad's known her so long, *his* first home was her belly.

"Eventually," Dad finally says.

More stuffy silence.

Then: "I'll finish making the arrangements once I've got you settled in. They'll release her from the hospital this afternoon. No charges have been filed against her—yet." He shakes his head.

If he only knew . . .

"I'm hoping they'll let us drive the camper back to Georgia. They'll likely confiscate it as soon as we get there because of—" Now his face is turning red. Which, oddly enough, makes Scoob grin just the slightest bit. *This* is the Dad he knows. Wound tighter than a yo-yo string. "Never mind, that's neither here nor there right now. Point being, we'll return to Atlanta, and your grandmother will stay with us until—"

He stops again.

"Until she's not there anymore," Scoob finishes.

"Yes. That. We'll make sure she's comfortable, and, uhh . . ."

Scoob watches the bump in Dad's neck move up and down, up and down. Like he's trying to swallow, speak, *something,* but can't.

Which, to Scoob, is fine.

He doesn't need to.

The drive back feels strange.

They are able to take the RV, and Dad hires a nurse to travel with them for G'ma's sake. She stays asleep in the back for most of the trip, but when she *is* awake, she's "lucid," as Scoob's heard the nurse refer to it. She doesn't say a whole lot to anyone—mostly just gazes out the window at the passing landscape—but the handful of times she and Scoob make eye contact, she smiles at him. Sadly, but still, it's a smile.

They make one extended stop back in Monroe, Louisiana, so G'ma can use a real restroom and Dad can catch a nap.

But of course Dad wants to talk first. As soon as G'ma and the nurse are gone, Dad comes and sits across from Scoob at the dining booth.

He doesn't say a word at first. Which is fine; Scoob can't get his eyes to lift past Dad's beard. Which is why he knows the exact moment Dad finds his words.

"I'm, uhh . . . well, I'll admit I'm not real good at this part," Dad says, and now Scoob does lift his eyes to Dad's because those certainly aren't the words he was expecting.

Dad takes a deep breath. "I'm glad you're okay, son," he continues. "I know I don't always do a great job of showing it, but you mean everything in the universe to me, William. I don't know what I'd do—" He shifts his focus to the ceiling. Starts rapid-fire blinking and doing that gulpy thing that makes his neck-bump look like a bouncing Ping-Pong ball.

Scoob's *never* seen Dad like this. Especially not when it comes to *him*. "I know I can be too hard on you, and I'm gonna try to be better about that. I just—when I couldn't get in touch with you-all . . . those were the worst seventy-two hours of my life, son."

Scoob's turn to gulp. "So you told the police I'd been kidnapped?"

"Huh?"

"On one of our stops, I saw this news report. There was an Amber Alert, and they said G'ma was also being investigated for a *string* of jewelry thefts."

"Ah," Dad says. "So you *do* know about all that." He tugs at his beard.

"Is it true?"

"What?"

"That she, uhh . . ." Scoob's roving gaze lands on G'ma's bed. It's almost like he can see her confession scrawled across the duvet. "Stole stuff."

Dad sighs. Sits up in his seat and narrows his eyes like he's been asking the same question. "I honestly couldn't tell you, son. Apparently there's some surveillance footage at one place, and enough evidence in another to make a connection. I can't definitively say she *didn't* do it . . . it's not uncommon for people to act rashly when they know they're coming to the end of life," he says. "She did sell her house, buy an RV, and take you across four state lines without alerting *either* of us to her sickness."

There's the old Dad. Hypercritical in the most low-key way possible.

"She *didn't* kidnap me," Scoob says with more slice in his tone than he intends. But since it's out there: "I left voluntarily." And just in case Dad isn't catching what Scoob's throwing, he adds, "I *wanted* to leave with her."

Scoob watches the verbal punches land and immediately wishes he could pull them all back.

"I didn't tell anyone you'd been kidnapped, William."

"Oh."

"I reported you both missing, but because of the other . . . *investigation*, they lumped the incidents together, decided it was possible you were in danger, and decided to treat it as a 'family abduction' case."

"And you didn't correct them?" Honestly, Scoob doesn't know why, of all the things, *this* is making him so mad.

Dad studies Scoob's face. "I'm going to tell you the truth even though it may make you even angrier with me," he says. "All right?"

Scoob nods.

"I didn't *know* that what they were suggesting was *in*correct, William. I saw the security footage captured at one of the four stores she's accused of stealing from, and—well, it's hard to deny it's her, son. I know the woman who raised me, but once I learned she was sick and hadn't told me—hadn't told *us*—I didn't know *what* she was capable of.

"I knew you likely weren't in any danger, and I also knew you left voluntarily and without coercion. What I didn't know was where you were going and for how long. Because she wouldn't tell me. And after she stopped answering the phone and wouldn't return my calls, I began to wonder whether or not she planned to bring you *back*."

Scoob doesn't respond. It's not like he knows these answers either.

"When I heard the phone had been *found* somewhere, I started assuming the worst—"

There's a knock, and then the main door opens, and Dad rises to assist G'ma up the RV stairs. G'ma blows Scoob a kiss in passing, and then the nurse helps G'ma get resettled into the bed. Scoob can see the slightly yellow tint to her skin, and every time she moves, it's clear her back hurts.

Once the curtain is drawn, Scoob expects Dad to sit back down across from him.

He doesn't.

In fact, he doesn't say a single word. Just returns to the cab, draws all the window shades, slides into the driver's seat, and reclines it to the limit.

Guess they could all use a little time.

Hopefully it's not more than they have.

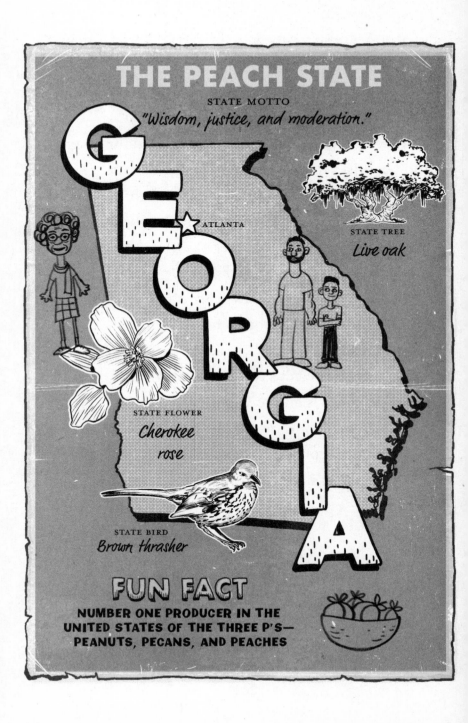

Good

They get seventeen more days.
Most of them good.

Going for a Drive

Scoob is strangely resolute as he and Dad return home from picking up the ashes. It was odd to him that there wouldn't be a funeral, but when Dad showed him the spot in G'ma's will where she requested for things to be this way, Scoob didn't ask questions. Just picked an urn made from the same type of wood as G'ma's treasure chest.

He glances over his shoulder at where that urn is sitting on the backseat. Dad didn't say a word as Scoob gingerly placed it there and strapped it in with the seat belt. It was the most Scoob felt like he could do. G'ma wasn't able to move or speak during her final four days of life, so Scoob's dream of strapping *her* into the car—in person, not ash form—so he and Dad could drive her past her old house can't ever come true. This will have to do.

Scoob rotates back forward and a surge of tears blurs his vision as Dad pulls up in front of the place. Dad puts the car in park.

There's a redheaded guy chasing a toddler around the yard. Which is newly fenced in. The house is also gray now where it was bright turquoise before.

It hits Scoob: this really *isn't* G'ma's house any-more.

The shakedown of her Winnebago didn't turn up anything other than the $42,520 Scoob saw in the space behind the TV. And since there was nothing overtly suspicious about it—"Children of folks who lived through the Depression are known for keep-ing large amounts of cash where they can see it," the detective said. "Our guess is this was her life savings"—the money *and* the RV, which G'ma had paid for in full, were both turned over to Dad.

He put the cash in a savings account for Scoob but hasn't decided what he'll do with good ol' *Senior* yet.

"I can't believe they painted the house," Dad says, wiping his own eyes again. "And that hideous bland gray, too. We should go and demand they change it back."

Scoob knows Dad's not entirely serious, but it does get his wheels turning: how much harder must it be for Dad to look at the house right now? It's the one *he* grew up in. And G'ma certainly didn't consult Dad before she sold it with all his memories inside.

"Hey, Dad?"

"Yeah, son?"

Scoob forces himself to look Dad in the eye. Then he puts a hand on Dad's shoulder. "I'm sorry you lost your mom."

At first Dad doesn't reply. Just nods. More tears run down his face.

Then, "I'm sorry too, William."

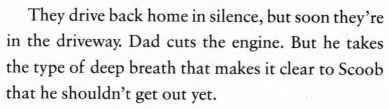

They drive back home in silence, but soon they're in the driveway. Dad cuts the engine. But he takes the type of deep breath that makes it clear to Scoob that he shouldn't get out yet.

"So I've been thinking," Dad says, and he doesn't have to say a single other word for Scoob to know exactly what he's been thinking about.

Scoob's been thinking too. A lot. And he already knows what he's going to say before Dad even asks the question Scoob knows is coming.

"I know I don't talk about your mother much— frankly, she's a . . . *painful* topic for me. Which I know is neither here nor there for *you*, but—"

He stops. Clenches his jaw.

Relaxes.

Resumes: "Point being, she *is* your mother. And she's been asking to see you, so if you'd like to meet her—"

"That's okay, Dad," Scoob says.

Dad's head whips right faster than Scoob can blink.

Scoob looks out the window. "Prolly sounds weird, but . . . I don't think I'm ready."

It's the *truest* thing he's said in days.

When there's no response, Scoob checks to make sure Dad heard him—and on Dad's face is a look of surprise more *pleasant* than Scoob expected. But oddly enough, Scoob thinks he gets it: Dad's not the only one in the car who knows something about a *mom* the other guy doesn't.

"Well, all right then," Dad says. "You'll let me know when you're ready, I presume?"

For the first time in days, Scoob *really* smiles. Feels good, this being-on-the-same-page thing. "Yeah, Dad," he says. "I will."

Scoob has no idea what prompts him to open G'ma's treasure chest and reexamine the contents three days later, but he's got everything spread out on the floor in his bedroom, and he's going through it all piece by piece.

He unfolds the Mexico map—which he hadn't done before—and is shocked to discover there's a second circle in addition to the one around Juárez. A city called Guaymas on the Gulf of California.

Puts it down and checks the Green Book again—*Playa de Cortés* is underlined beneath *Guaymas*. Scoob has no idea how he missed it.

His eyes rove over everything else on the floor and hook onto the necklace with the key charm. Scoob smiles: he laid it out the exact way G'ma did in Mississippi.

He carefully picks up the thin gold chain. Turns it over. Rubs a thumb over the key, then holds it up to the light; squints at it.

His eyes drop to the treasure box.

Laying the necklace back down, Scoob picks up the wooden chest and takes it over to his desk so he can get a better look at it under the light of his lamp. Despite feeling like he's desecrating a holy relic, he flips it over and runs a hand along the bottom. Feels all the grooves and edges. Looks more closely at the sides. Holds it close to his ear and gives it a shake.

Nothing.

Still, though . . .

He sets it down and lifts the lid. Traces his fingers over the velvet interior, sides, back, bottom—

There's a bump—a *tab,* it seems—against the front interior wall, just behind where the latch sits on the outside.

Scoob wedges a fingernail behind it and tugs until a little flap pops open.

Revealing a small hole beneath.

Scoob looks over his shoulder at the gaping entrance to his bedroom. Dad's loosened up a bit since they got back home, but the *No Closed Doors* policy still stands. Hopefully the guy doesn't decide to come upstairs in the next couple minutes. . . .

Because Scoob grabs the necklace and pushes the little key down into the exposed hole in the box.

Perfect fit.

He turns it—

And the bottom of the box *pops* open, revealing a folded sheet of white paper with *William Armando "Scoob-a-doob" Lamar* scribbled on the outside.

And when Scoob takes *that* out, he uncovers enough shiny, sparkly, glittery stuff to *surely* pay for college, buy him a car, and maybe get him a decent-sized house, too.

There are necklaces, bracelets, earrings—a pair of pink diamonds included—*brutches* or *broochets* or whatever the heck those weird bedazzly things with the safety pins on the back are called. All strapped down and/or tucked into weird cushioned crevasses.

He unfolds the note.

You're a good egg, Scoob-a-doob. Don't ever let anyone tell you different. Thank you for your impeccable wingman service to this old lady on her final adventure.
 Love you forever.
 G'ma

Quick as he can, Scoob shuts the hidden compartment, locks it, conceals the keyhole, and runs from his room.

"Dad!" he says, practically throwing himself

down the stairs. He skids around the corner and into the living room.

"Whoa, son, where's the fire?"

"Dad, we gotta go on a trip!"

One of Dad's thick eyebrows shoots up, and Scoob looks at the urn on the mantel.

Dad follows his focus.

They hold this position for who knows how long—Dad sitting in his chair, Scoob standing beside it, both staring at what remains of Ruby Jean Lamar, mother, grandmother, wife, pilferer of jewels—then look back at each other.

Dad nods. "I'll book us a flight."

But Scoob shakes his head.

"No?" Dad says.

Scoob doesn't reply. He knows there's no need to.

Dad returns his gaze to the urn and sighs.

Smiles sadly.

"Guess we're going for a drive."

Clean Getaway

Dad's a good sport.

He lets Scoob navigate the whole trip from his map, and they make the same stops so Dad can see all Scoob and G'ma got up to on their *adventuring*.

Dad doesn't ask questions when Scoob leads him to a jewelry store in Mississippi so Scoob can "give something to a guy named Todd." Nor does he bat an eyelash when Scoob requests a gas station stop in Shreveport to deliver hand-drawn cards to a pair of workers that say *Thanks for the Anonymous Tip*.

They don't make any stops at all on the almost-four-hour stretch between Monahans, Texas—

where Scoob and G'ma's trip ended—and Ciudad Juárez in Chihuahua, Mexico. But it takes another half day for them to reach Guaymas.

Dad doesn't say a word as Scoob grabs his backpack and heads down the beach toward the water. Just stares into the campfire he and Scoob built together from scratch. The RV is parked back at Hotel Playa de Cortés—which Scoob was relieved to find had been renovated since G'ma and G'pop tried to get to it in 1968—and he knows Dad is tired from all the driving, so he wants to make this part quick.

After finding a little cove beneath a small rock formation that juts out over the water, Scoob looks

around to make sure no one's watching him, then drops to his hands and knees and gets to work.

Once the hole is wide and deep enough, Scoob pulls G'ma's treasure box—wrapped in about twenty-seven layers of plastic wrap and full of everything that was already in there, plus the Green Book and Scoob's map, which he added as soon as they parked—out of his backpack, and before he can think too much about it, he sets it down in the hole and shoves the dirt back over it.

"Finally made it, G'ma," he says.

Then after a quick swipe at his eyes, Scoob stands. And he smiles.

"You made a clean getaway."

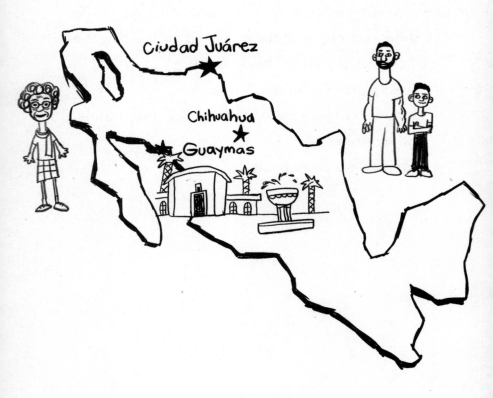

Acknowledgments

For such a short book, this one was truly a labor of love. Thanks to the following people for helping me bring it to life:

My beloved Nigel, your commitment to *my* dreams—as evidenced by the care you give our sons and our home while I'm off in a Starbucks typing away or on the road talking about the stuff I typed—is genuinely the only reason I'm able to do any of this. I intend to eventually buy you a jet similar to the one Beyoncé got for Jay-Z. That way you can fly as far away from children and laundry as possible when the mood strikes you.

Phoebe Yeh. Editor, yes, but also mom and guide and encourager and caretaker and Book-Nana and friend. Your belief in me and my abilities makes me want to prove you right.

Jason Reynolds is the person who was originally like "Yo, you *can* do middle-grade. Don't overthink it. It's writing about kids *preparing* for the stuff they'll face in YA novels." For that little push—and every single one before and since—I am forever grateful and indebted. (Also: lemme hold $20.)

Dhonielle Clayton: there would be no Green Book in this novel without you mentioning it that one time we were at RT and going to Jenny Han's room. Thank you for the introduction to the thing that literally gave this book a central theme.

William Armando Lamar Sr., cousin extraordinaire: 'preciate you letting me borrow that most excellent name of yours. And same to Ms. Ruby Jean Truman (and her mom, Joanna Truman). You, dear pup, have officially been immortalized in human form.

To my children, Kiran and Milo, who sometimes let me work and who thank me for all the toys I buy them as a result. I love you little turkeys.

Thanks also to my parents (Big Mil and TB) and siblings (Marc and Brina) and all the sweet baby children I've had the privilege of interacting with on school visits that inspired this novel and helped me with lingo. To Rena Rossner for believing in this book (and SELLING IT). And to my ever-supportive friends who listened to me complain while I worked on it: Octavia, Tiffany, Ashley, Angie, Brittany, Tanya, Dede, Vera, Matt, Chisom, Joey, Lamar, Jeff, and Greg.

My Random House honey bunnies: Elizabeth, Kathy, Barbara, Felicia, John (nemesis!), Dominique, Judith, Jules, Sydney, Adrienne, Lisa, and K-Schizzle.

And to my most favoritest middle school teacher loves and librarians: Adrian Stallings, Adrian Pickworth, Sarah

Bonner, Drew Shilhanek, Olukemi Kamson, Korey Collins, Anna Bernstein, Wyatt Oroke, Toni Rose Deanon, Ashleigh Rose, Mary Thomas, Kelli Monedero, and Travis Crowder. Thank you for all that you infuse into the next generation. Your students are #blessed (and so am I to know you!).

Lastly, to my own granny, Glenda Alexander: You might not be an international jewel thief, but you're still the truest OG.

About the Author

NIC STONE is an Atlanta native and a Spelman College graduate. After working extensively in teen mentoring and living in Israel for several years, she returned to the United States to write full-time. Nic's debut novel for young adults, *Dear Martin*, was a *New York Times* bestseller and William C. Morris Award finalist. She is also the author of the teen titles *Odd One Out*, a novel about discovering oneself and who it is okay to love, which was an NPR Best Book of the Year and a Rainbow Book List Top Ten selection, and *Jackpot*, a love-*ish* story that takes a searing look at economic inequality.

Clean Getaway, Nic's first middle-grade novel, deals with coming to grips with the pain of the past and facing the humanity of our heroes. She lives in Atlanta with her adorable little family.

nicstone.info